ROSEBRIAR

Maudie Gunier

Order this book online at www.trafford.com
or email orders@trafford.com

Most Trafford titles are also available at major online book retailers.

Printed in the United States of America.

ISBN: 978-1-4269-5319-4 (sc)
ISBN: 978-1-4269-5320-0 (e)

Trafford rev. 01/27/2011

 www.trafford.com

North America & international
toll-free: 1 888 232 4444 (USA & Canada)
phone: 250 383 6864 ◆ fax: 812 355 4082

CHAPTER 1

Fall 1979

Maggie watched from her second story bedroom window as Jess Morgan got out of his white medical pickup and disappeared into the barn. Perhaps she had better go down to the barn and see if she could offer her help. She had no idea what he was here for, as none of the animals were sick as far as she knew, but presumed Bill had probably wanted him to check one of them.

She didn't mind breaking away from the fall cleaning in the bedroom and enjoyed talking to Dr. Morgan when he wasn't in his usual hurry. She knew he was busy from early dawn to way past dark almost seven days a week. With only two veterinarians in the rural farm area they were both over work.

She glanced at herself in the dresser mirror, smoothing her disarrayed dark blond hair, which she usually wore in a tasseled mass of curls to her shoulders, but had pulled it back from her face into a bun to clean house today. She wiped a smudge of dirt from beneath one deep blue eye, rolled her jean legs down, and grabbed a sweatshirt, slipping it on as she hurried down the stairs. "Good day, Jess, what brings you out here on a Saturday afternoon?"

"Hi, Maggie, Bill called earlier and wanted me to take a look at this calf. I'm going to give him some shots. He doesn't look very sick now, but if it isn't better by tomorrow I'll need to get some bloating medication down him. Will you be here tomorrow?"

"Sure, if you need me to help."

"Well, I could use some help holding him, and Bill said he would be gone today and tomorrow," Jess said, as he filled a syringe with clear liquid. "I'll call Bill early in the morning before he leaves to see how the calf is doing, and then call you later if I'm coming out."

"Sure that will be fine, Doctor," Maggie answered.

"How's the clothing business doing?" he asked, as he pushed the calf up against the wall of the barn, holding him there while he pushed the needle into his hip.

"Oh just fine. My two employees keep after me to hire more help. So I'm thinking about moving into a shop in town where we would have more room for the sewing equipment," she answered, as she took hold of the calf's head so that he could get a second shot into the neck.

"Sounds like you have a winner there. Go for it, Maggie. Wilcottville needs another clothing store. Would you also buy from other clothing companies or could you make all your own designs?"

Maggie laugh, "Well, I'm afraid we couldn't make enough for an entire store, but I would carry a lot of own designs."

Dr. Morgan seemed unhurried today and prompted conversation. "I've thought about building a larger clinic on the outskirts of town, but can't seem to find the time to take care of the business end of it. I'm waiting for the real estate to call me on some property that I looked at, than maybe my attorney can handle the sale and some of the construction."

"Everything does take time. But we certainly could use a larger animal clinic in this area." Maggie stated and changed the subject. "I haven't seen Adrian for awhile. How is she doing, Jess?"

Dr. Morgan turned his attention away from the calf, and they walked out of the barn together.

"She's doing fine. She has her good days and bad days. Complains that I work too much and I'm not home enough," he smiled at Maggie, "but in my business I have to work day and night. I'll probably be by tomorrow to doctor that calf," he said as he got into his pickup and drove down the long driveway to the road.

Maggie watched him pull out onto the country road on to his next appointment. She didn't know much about Jess Morgan's life except that he was one of the best veterinarians for miles around. His wife, Adrian, was badly injured in a car accident about eight years ago, just before they moved to this area. The accident had left her paralyzed from the waist down. Maggie heard this had left her bitter and resentful toward life. Dr. Morgan never talked much about his wife and seemed to keep his personal life to himself. With his good looks and outgoing personality Maggie imagined there were a lot of lonely ranch wives seeking his attention, but she never heard any gossip among her friends. What did a healthy middle aged man do when his wife was paralyzed—or could he have a mistress somewhere that no one knew about? Maggie found him attractive, and he was always friendly, but never to the point of flirting with her. He was respectful and kept his distance as though he tried to avoid being too close to her.

She looked toward her huge white colonial style home, not wanting to go up and finish the fall cleaning in her bedroom. It was a beautiful Indian summer day, too nice to be inside. She glanced again down the long drive way with its rows of Blue Spruce trees and climbing roses on each side. She felt restless inside and decided to walk a ways through the orchard where the red and golden leaves waved gently in the breeze.

The walnuts had been knocked and picked up already, as were the apples harvested from the adjoining orchard. She was glad the harvest work was over early this year, but she almost dreaded the long winter months that stretched ahead. She had never felt this way before. She had always looked forward to the seasons, especially the anticipation of the Thanksgiving and Christmas holidays. Could it be she didn't want to get older. She would be hitting forty in January, the half way mark in life.

She stopped walking, reaching up she touched a leaf hanging from a small thin branch. The dried leaf fell slowly to the ground. She looked around at the beauty of the golden leaf walnut trees. The birds were noisily chirping at this intruder who dare to walk in their peaceful environment.

Why did she feel like she wanted to lay down here and sleep forever. To blot out her life. To blot out Bill and the children. She had so much to live for, but yet this feeling of gloom she felt so often lately engulfed her whole being. The tears welled up in her eyes. She couldn't stop feeling sorry for herself, yet she didn't know why. She dropped down on a pile of dried leaves beneath a tree, leaning her back against the trunk she drew her long slender legs up, crossing one over the other. Why had life become to complicated lately. She had everything to live for. A husband she had been married to for twenty some years and two lovely children.

Julie's wedding would be in a few weeks and Jonathan's graduation from law school in several years, and probably some grandchildren to look forward to later on. Bill was a hard working husband and he loved her. She had a beautiful comfortable home and this land with its orchards and fields and cattle. Not only did she have all this, but also a promising career in leather clothing design. What more could she want ?

Maggie turned over on her side. Picking up a leaf she twirled the stem between her fingers. She and Bill had come a long way since their wedding day. Her folks had given them three hundred acres for a wedding present and later gave them the family homestead, Rosebriar, which was built by Maggie's grandfather. They had bought nine hundred acres adjoining it, where they raised cattle and planted hay. Her parents had retired because of her father's ill health and moved into town.

Maggie and Bill had worked hard those first years, especially when they planted the orchards. The young tender trees had to have a lot of care, with the right amount of water, fertilizer and spray. After the trees matured they worked long hours through the spring and summer up until the last harvest. Now that they could afford more help in the orchards and with the cattle, Maggie devoted most of her time to her clothing business.

Bill was a good husband. She had few complaints. Some things she would like to change about him, but doesn't everyone have complaints about their marital partner, she thought. There was something missing in her life though. If only the passion she desired with Bill was there. The desire to touch him and to be touched by him. To feel her heart flutter at his smile. Was it there once? Maybe a long time ago, so long ago...it seemed to never have existed. She didn't stop loving him, but had lost interest in their relationship. It was his uncaring ways, although she knew that he really did care. But in Bill's quiet manner he failed to tell her of his love, to possess her the way she wanted to be possessed. In bed he was not the lover she longed for. The first few years of marriage he proved he could be romantic at times, but as the years passed he seemed to forget that Maggie

4

too had desires and needed fulfillment as much as he did. The love for his work of the land and cattle seemed to consume all his time, his very soul. He was driven to perfection when it came to that.

Maggie had always been a warm lovable wife to Bill and had encouraged him in more passionate love making, but she finally gave up, hiding her feelings. Bill still enjoyed sex, but the silly foreplay of it seemed to embarrass him now, and he just wanted to quickly get it over with, leaving Maggie so many times flustered that she dreaded it when Bill reached for her in bed. There were many times she would wake up through the night and lay there, her breast aching to be caressed, to feel the touch of lips on her nipples, but she learned to suppress these feelings and work harder in her career and on the ranch, so that she was exhausted at bedtime. It was something she had learned to live with, and Bill was so kind and good in other ways, she couldn't help but love him all these years.

It was beginning to turn dusk. The setting sun turned the western sky a fluffy pink. Maggie was just getting to her feet when the two Brittany Spaniels ran up jumping on her, knocking her back into a sitting position. She laugh, forgetting her depression, "Hello, Sissy and Boy, where have you two been all day, chasing squirrels? Guess we had better go home, so I can start dinner. It's the cook's day off."

Off in the distance an owl hooted its enlightenment to the approaching darkness as Maggie walked toward home. She remembered how Julie and Jonathan use to follow the owls when they were little. My God! Where did the years go. The kids are grown. The years flew by after they started high school. Julie was a cheerleader and joined the Junior Club of Maggie's women's club. Jonathan played football and belonged to F.F.A. . These among other activities they were both involved in made the years swiftly pass by, too fast as far as Maggie was concerned. She would like to relive the children's high school years. They were precious years, with not too many problems as far as teenagers were concerned. Most of her friends had far more problems with their teens than her and Bill.

She would never forget the hurt in Jonathan's voice the one time they had to pick him up at the police station when he and a young boyfriend were picked up with an open beer bottle in the car. The parents were called and a lecture by two policemen were given to the boys. As Maggie cried softly all the way home and Bill lectured, Jonathan repeated over and over "I'm sorry Mom, I'm sorry Mom." Now he was grown and would someday be an attorney.

Julie's wedding was planned for the first part of December. All the wedding plans were made. The wedding gown and attendants dresses that Maggie, her mother and Julie had been working so hard on were almost finished. Now if she didn't forget to send the invitations, everything should go smoothly. Maggie only wished she could be more excited about the wedding. But after all, her only daughter was leaving home. There would be no more mother-daughter talks after Julie came home from a date. No more cooking or making homemade jelly in the kitchen together or walks through the orchard.

Maggie adored Julie's future husband, Steve. She could not have chosen a more suitable husband for Julie herself. He was not a "total babe", as the young people refer to the good looking ones of this generation, but he was handsome in a mild sort of way, and had the charm and personality of a prince.

He teased Maggie almost as much as he did Julie when they were all together, and he had a lovable way about him that Maggie hoped would make a lasting marriage for the young couple. They would live in Sacramento after the wedding and Julie would continue her college to become a speech therapist. Steve already had his career established with his father's rubber manufacturing business there.

Maggie knew her depression was more than Julie moving away from home. It was herself, what was she going to do with her life. She had an exciting career, but yet she felt something was missing. It wasn't exactly restlessness, but like a heavy burden eating away inside. She wanted to cry, but the tears would not come. A feeling to runaway, to escape, often came over her, but she was too tired to run. The only thing that helped sometime was sleep, to escape for a short time. She craved sleep, but a lot of the time after going to bed she lay there tossing and turning.

She knew she had to pull herself out of this deep depression, but did she have the strength? She knew she should see a psychiatrist, but there was none in the small town of Wilcottville. She would have to drive over fifty miles to Sacramento, which she was use to in her business sometimes, but doctor appointments would have to be scheduled often, and she didn't really have the time. Was this an excuse she wondered. She stopped walking and leaned her head against a tree. Tears welled in her eyes.

"God, what's wrong with me. Why can't I be satisfied with my life?" She asked out loud. After a short time she started walking home . She hoped the red puffiness would be gone by the time she reached home, because Bill knew nothing of her depression. She didn't know why she hadn't told him. Maybe it was just too personal. He would only tell her to go see a doctor.

Bill was home when she returned. He looked rather strangely at her and she knew her eyes must still be a little red. "Hi, Mag, were you out walking?" He asked, with no mention about her eyes.

"Yes, I took a walk with the dogs. How was your day?"

"Oh, as good as can be expected. One of the machines broke down yesterday and I had to go to the city to get a part for it. I had to fire one of the Mexican workers yesterday. Julio just won't leave the alcohol alone. He's going to get someone hurt on that machinery. He was drunk again and broke the shaker."

A sad expression crossed Maggie's face, "That's ashamed. It's almost Christmas and he has six children. What will they do?" She asked more to herself than to Bill.

"I'm sorry Meg; but it couldn't be helped. I've given him five chances in the last two and a half months. He just won't leave the liquor alone and gets too careless. He doesn't want to do a good days work."

"But did you talk to him, Bill. Did you tell him last time that he only had one more chance?" she asked.

"Maggie, I've told him and told him not to be so careless and to quit drinking when he's on the job. There's only another two weeks of work anyway, and I would have to lay him off. He can draw his unemployment a few weeks early. I'll say he was laid off. Not for him, but for his wife and kids."

They were both quiet for awhile. "Well, maybe the Christmas basket should go to his family this year," Maggie said, "I don't have another family in mind yet anyway. Not that I'm condoning his behavior, Bill, but I do feel sorry for his family. With six children they won't get much for Christmas."

"Sure Meg , why not. You make the decision on that."

She knew Bill could care less where the Christmas basket went. That was the least of his worries. The basket was a tradition that had been passed down from Maggie's grandmother to her mother and now her, and she hoped Julie would carry it on someday. The basket was filled with a large turkey and ham, cranberries, dressing mix, celery, cream cheese, oranges, apples, cookies and candy and anything else for a traditional Christmas dinner along with a large box of wrapped toys for the children. The basket was delivered the day before Christmas by a mysterious messenger to a needy family in their area.

A few years ago the news media got wind of the mysterious Christmas basket and had tried to find out who the responsible Santa's helper was, but their efforts were aimless, and it was still a kept family secret that no one outside of Maggie's family knew. The family didn't want praise or glory for this, they only wanted to make a needy family happy at Christmas.

"Oh hon," Bill said, as though he remembered something important to tell her. Maggie jumped as he interrupted her thoughts, which drifted back from the basket.

"Did Dr. Morgan attend to the sick calf today?"

"Yes, he gave it two shots, and he's going to call you early tomorrow to see how the calf is doing," she answered.

Maggie hung onto the two hundred and fifty pound calf as tightly as she could. Dr. Morgan was on the other side with his arm around the calf's neck. With one hand he held the funnel and tube going into the calf's mouth and with his other hand he poured the mixed mineral oil and bloating medicine down the funnel.

His smooth tanned neck and broad shoulders were muscled from constant wrestling with the animals he worked on. His slightly graying hair complimented his tan and made him even more handsome than he was.

The veterinarian pulled the tube out and the calf lunged swinging Maggie directly into Dr. Morgan. He caught her to keep her from falling and held her tightly as her eyes met his. He slowly drew her closer and lightly kissed her on the lips. Maggie couldn't pull away from him. He was like a magnetic force pulling her closer. He held her tighter and kissed her again, harder this time, while Maggie responded with a passion to match his. He released her almost as suddenly as he had caught her.

"I'm sorry, Maggie, I didn't mean for that to happen. It's just that," He hesitated for a few moments, "I've been attracted to you for a long time. Well, damn it, Maggie," he said, lowering his eyes to the ground, avoiding her eyes like a love stricken teenager, "I've been in love with you for a long time." He slowly looked into her eyes, "Now you know how I feel."

Maggie stood there, still weak and speechless, knowing that he cared for her, while she had felt something for him in the past months, but didn't want to admit it. God, what were they getting into, she thought. She knew what Jess Morgan's life at home must be like. But did he really love her?

"Maggie," Jess said, shocking her back into reality. "Where do we go from here?"

"I guess I've cared for you to, Jess," she slowly said, "without really realizing it was happening, but I don't know where to go from here. We're both married, we have obligations to others. Let's try to let it stop here, Jess."

"I know you're right, but I also sense that you're not happy either. I won't push you, Maggie, but it's going to be hard to be around you after this and not able to touch you."

He gave Maggie instructions on caring for the calf and walked to his truck with his head down. He looked sad as he waved to her and drove off down the driveway. Maggie leaned against the barn and did not try to hold back the tears and sobs that shook her body. She knew her protected life was changing and she had feelings for Jess that could win out in the end.

In the weeks that followed she tried to keep Jess out of her thoughts, and threw herself entirely into her work, designing some of her best leather creations she had ever made, and making the final plans for Julie's wedding.

She was strong enough that she kept her depression at a low key, motivating herself to think only of her career and future plans for it.

Her designs took on new dimension. One she liked best was a vest, a little longer than the usual vest designs she had done before, and it could be worn by the larger women. She already had three orders for it in large sizes. She also was working on a brief case, something new she was getting into, to go along with the purse line.

She knew she would have to find a shop in town large enough for the business, but she had looked at the only three available and they were all too small. Her work shop at home was once the large parlor. The windows in the room faced the east, and Maggie liked to start work early in the morning with the sun shining into the room, warming it and providing extra light to cut and sew with. Three heavy duty sewing machines were set up in the room, with plenty of space for each person a separate work area. Several cutting boards were laid out, an ironing board pulled out from a wall, and shelves and a storage area had been built for material and supplies.

The two ladies that Maggie employed to help her with the leather sewing were complaining of the eight hour work days lately. They had been use to working six hours a day. She was contemplating hiring a third women so that all three could only work a six hour day. Sewing for three hours in the morning and three in the afternoon was enough, and she understood how her employees felt.

She disliked the thought of interviewing for a new employee because it took up valuable time, but she wouldn't use an employment agency, even though an agency had called her twice this month to see if she needed their services. Since she had to make the final decision of the hiring anyway, she felt an agency a waste of time.

Maggie also traveled a lot showing her designs to her customers and contacting new stores to see if they would be interested in carrying "Designs By Meg." Her travels took her to stores in Sacramento, San Francisco and around the Bay area. She had thought about venturing into Southern California, but there would be time for that later when she had more employees to do the sewing. She had given a lot of thought to hiring a sales agent, but she loved the travel and knew she could represent her leather designs better than anyone else. Things were moving so fast and the business was rapidly growing, that Maggie knew sooner or later she would have to hire an agent and move into larger quarters.

Most of her time now was spent on Julie's upcoming wedding, which was only two weeks away. The invitations were out to almost everyone in Wilcottville. It seemed the older town families that Maggie and Bill had grown up with, and the younger generation of Julie and Steve's friends. Two large subdivisions had gone up in the last three years, and a lot of new people had moved into the town.

An invitation had been sent to Dr. And Mrs. Jess Morgan. With everyone else of importance coming it would look odd if the town veterinarian and his wife were not invited. Maggie knew Adrian loved parties and rarely missed any, even though she was bound to a wheel chair. Sometimes she would come alone with her nurse, if her husband was working or out of town.

Maggie turned the dial on the sewing machine to set it for the monogram stitching. She had to get her mind on this sewing if she was going to get it finished before the customer came to pick the skirt up.

"I'm going to put a fresh pot of coffee on. Maybe it will help me to concentrate better, " she told her employees, Alice and Jennifer, as she left the room.

"Maggie, I'm having trouble with this tuck...I think we're going to have to redesign this pattern a little," Alice said, as Maggie walked back into the sewing room and examined the piece of leather material in which Alice was working with.

"I think you're right," she said as she glanced over her glasses at her slightly plump employee. "I see here what the problem is, but I have to get this other order finished before the customer gets here to pick it up at five."

"Maggie is something troubling you lately?" The older women asked with concern. "You seem to be a million miles away at times when you're in here working with us."

Maggie glanced around the room, "By the way, where is Jennifer? Did she leave?"

"Yes, she remembered she had a dentist appointment and said to tell you she would be back in the morning."

"Oh, okay. Alice, have you been married a long time?" Maggie inquisitively asked.

Alice laugh, "Does this have something to do with your problem?"

"No, but I really don't know much about you except that you're married to a very nice man and you have four grown children and seven grandchildren. But you're what, sixty four, so haven't you had problems along the way?"

"Sure, everyone I ever knew has some kind of problem. Sometimes it seems like everyone else hasn't a care in the world until you really get to know them and find out the hard times they are going through or have went through. I've been married three times, Maggie, so you know I've had problems," she laughed. "My first husband died at a very young age. He was only thirty-four, and we were so much in love. He had cancer, and after we found out it was just a matter of months until he was gone. He's the father of my four children."

"That must have been very hard on you, Alice. I didn't realized you had to go through anything like that."

"I was thirty-eight when I remarried five years later, but that was a bad choice I found out a few months after the wedding. That husband beat me and abused my kids. We stuck it out for almost two years, but it was a good thing I got out of that marriage when I did before it damaged my kids permanently. After that I raised the children alone and took in sewing and ironing, which made us a pretty good living for those times. I vowed that I wouldn't even think of remarrying until the kids were all out of college or married, and sometimes I felt like I never wanted to get married again. But after the kids were on their own," Alice went on, "along came good ole Fred and he is truly a sweetheart, the kind of husband every woman should have. I only wish I would have met him when my kids were still little."

"Yes, Fred is really one in a million, " Maggie offered.

"Now what is bothering you, Maggie? Do you want to talk about it?"

"Oh, well nothing really, " she hesitated, "It's just that Bill and I have a solid marriage, but it isn't really a happy one. Not for a long time anyway.

I feel like," she hesitated again, "Well like I'm missing something, Alice. I'll soon be forty, and I feel like I haven't lived yet. Like I'm missing the fun times a wife and husband should have together. Just the little things–like talking in bed at night, or walking hand in hand together through the park. It's never been that way, Alice, and I want that."

"Have you ever talked to Bill about this?"

"A long time ago, but all he cares about is his orchards and the land and cattle. I love him, Alice, and I know he loves me, but something is gone out of that love that I don't think can ever be renewed.

"But, Maggie, you have so much. Don't throw what you have away because you miss holding hands and giggling in bed."

"I know you're right, Alice, but I can't help feeling like I've missed out on something special all my life and I need to do something about it. Oh look at the time," she said, glancing at her watch. "I have to get this order finished by five." Maggie walked across the large room to her sewing machine, but her thoughts were on her confused life.

CHAPTER 2

The usher seated Maggie in her reserved mother-of-the-bride seat. She was overwhelmed at the large crowd of about three hundred people that filled the huge church, Even though she had sent out the invitations. The church seemed packed to its capacity and then some. She ran her hand over the front of her rose colored Edwardian gown as she sat alone waiting for the wedding music to begin. She was determined not to be sad today. This was one of the happiest days in her daughter's life and she would only cry tears of joy. She wished that the music would begin. She wasn't use to setting alone in front of three hundred people, who Maggie felt about half of the crowd's eyes were focused on her while they waited for the bridal party to begin walking down the aisle.

She smiled at her parents and Bill's where they sat at the other end of her pew, as her mother-in-law waved her hanky at Maggie. Her attention focused on the beautiful large flower arrangements in white baskets at the church altar. She was so close she could catch a scent of the light and dark pink Roses that were mixed with burgundy Elegant Baby Carnations, white and rubium Lilies and fern.

Maggie wondered if Jess Morgan and his wife were here. She hadn't seen him since he kissed her, the day the calf pushed her against him. She tried not to think of him over the past month, but little things about him kept slipping into her mind as she worked. She had worked with him a lot over the years doctoring the animals on her ranch. She had always been attracted to him, but never dared to think he may care anything about her.

The magnificent pipe organ filled the church with music that began the procession, and Maggie drifted back to where she was sitting as the four attendants came down the aisle in their dophne rose Victorian gowns on the arms of their escorts in burgundy tuxedos.

The wedding march began after the rest of the bridal party took their places at the front of the church. Maggie stood and leaned forward to see Julie as she came down the aisle on her father's arm. The glow on her face told Maggie how happy her daughter was, although Bill wasn't smiling, and looked terrified as every eye in the church focused on him and Julie.

Julie was beautiful in her white Victorian gown with the long chapel train which they had labored so hard to make. It looked elegant and went well with the brim hat trailing it's long vail behind. It seemed like forever before Bill placed Julie at the side of her bridegroom and sat down by Maggie. He patted her hand seeing that she was close to tears. She smiled and touched his hand softly. This was a special day for both of them. The wedding of their only daughter.

The past two weeks had been so frantic that Maggie was beginning to feel the exhaustion after the wedding, but she had to keep going to continue through the reception. The buffet dinner was catered to the reception hall and Maggie's friends insisted on taking care of all the details at the reception which left Maggie and Bill free to mingle with their guests.

The music from the young band was fantastic, and couples were already out on the dance floor. Maggie had insisted that whatever band Julie and Steve chose, they had to play some slow music also for the older guests to dance to. Maggie loved to dance, but Bill thought it looked ridiculous, and claimed his legs were to long and spindly.

"Maggie dear, that band is really good. Are they friends of your children?"

Maggie turned, slowly focusing her eyes downward on Adrian Morgan with Dr. Morgan behind her wheel chair. "Yes, Adrian, they're friends of the kids. How are you?" she asked, smiling at Adrian and then glancing at Jess as his eyes met hers.

Adrian didn't seem to notice and continued talking. "I'm doing as well as can be under the circumstances. We didn't stay at the church to offer our congratulations because it's so hard to get around among a lot of people, but—" she held her arms out to Maggie, as Maggie bent down to her level, "Congratulations dear. It was a beautiful wedding. One of the most prestigious I've ever seen in Wilcottville."

"Yes, it was lovely and Julie is a beautiful bride," Dr. Morgan said, as he lightly kissed her on the cheek, "congratulations."

"Thank you, thank you both. I'm so glad you could come," she smiled while her stomach fluttered from being so close to Jess.

"Adrian, you look very well and lovely as usual," Maggie said, trying to keep a calm voice. She wondered what had made Jess fall in love with his wife. She was pretty enough, with her short dark hair brushed toward her thin face, but she always thought Adrian to have an unpleasant personality. Kind of moody and sulky, kind of spoiled it seemed. She knew Adrian had always looked down on the less fortunate people of Wilcottville from things she had heard her say at some of their club meetings. Maggie had never been very good friends with her, just acquaintances, because they belonged to the same women's organization.

"Why thank you my dear. Oh Jess, there's Hazel Pentel, I must talk to her about something," she said, as she stirred her electric wheel chair toward her friend.

"Maggie, you look lovely too. Would you like to dance?" Jess asked with a pleading look in his eyes.

"Jess, I _____," Maggie hesitated, "Well, sure, Jess, why not."

The band was playing an old tune that was popular in the fifties. Jess held her gently in his arms, pulling her closer after awhile.

"I know we agreed to stay away from each other, but I love you," he whispered. "God forbid, Maggie, I can't stay away from you."

Maggie didn't answer. She seemed to float in his arms. She had visualized being held this way by Jess, but she knew she had to fight this urge to wrap her arms around him and be drowned in their passion. Instead she braced herself. Remembering that she was at her daughter's wedding with a huge room full of people watching. It was dark in the dance area and Maggie hoped no one saw his lips brush her neck, lingering there for a few moments. The darkness seemed to heighten every sensation.

"Jess, please, do you know what you're doing?" Maggie whispered as low as possible. "We shouldn't be dancing together."

"Alright, we'll do it your way. I'll wait for you for as long as you want. But please don't make me wait too long. I need you," he begged, as he leaned back looking at her with a hunger in his eyes that Maggie could see even in the dim lit room.

They continue dancing normally while her fingers felt the steel firmness of his back and shoulders through his dark suit coat. He still had the youthful body of a young man. Her body ached for him, but she could not give into its demands. They only danced once more with each other through-out the evening. They hardly talked, but just held each other, enjoying this new happiness of being in love, but scared at what the future may hold. She felt Jess' eyes on her more than once the rest of the evening, and the few times she had a chance to glance at him he smiled knowingly of their secret love.

Christmas was drawing near and Maggie's gift list was finally getting smaller, even though she had not had much time for shopping. She still had to find gifts for her two employees, Alice and Jennifer, and decided to shop for their gifts in Sacramento after she had delivered a jacket to a customer there. The Christmas orders for her leather designs were all finished and Maggie had the rest of the holiday to shop, bake and visit. Things she rarely had time for. Her employees were grateful for the time off too, and the three of them had agreed to meet for a holiday luncheon and exchange presents at the Riverside Log, a new restaurant in Wilcottville.

She picked up a silk scarf and thought of Jennifer, who had become one of her best friends this year. They found that they had a lot in common. Jennifer was just two years younger and did oil painting as a hobby as Maggie did.. She also loved to ride horses and they always talked of going horseback riding together someday.

Maggie laid the scarf back down and decided she would first pick out a blouse and match the scarf to it. She looked through the racks of expensive blouses searching for a blouse of the right color, with the proper neckline and bodice for a scarf. She had no idea what to get Alice. Alice was a good employee and hardly ever left a piece of sewing that was not completely finished. She was a perfectionist like Maggie when it came to putting out top quality sewing, and Maggie knew she was fortunate to have someone like that. Jennifer was a good seamstress now, but Maggie and Alice both worked hard at helping her become a better one.

"Oh, this is perfect," Maggie commented to herself, as she looked at a beige blouse with long sleeves, thinking how perfect it would go with the coco brown and beige stripped scarf. Now what to get Alice the thought, and decided a beautiful night gown and robe would be an excellent choice for her. She would also be giving both of them a bonus along with the gifts. A lovely baby blue gown and robe was chosen for Alice as Maggie knew blue was her favorite color. The clerk stapled the sack closed with the receipt, a policy some stores had that Maggie hated, but never the less it was one more small problem to live with Maggie was thinking, as she whirled around bumping directly into a man, knocking one of his many packages out of his arms.

"Oh, I'm very sorry," she said, swooping the package up handing it to him as she met his eyes.

"We seem to have a lot of collisions with each other," he smiled, and Maggie blushed.

"Jess, you must think I'm the clumsiest person in the world."

"I won't if you'll have a cup of coffee with me."

"Well, I guess I can have a cup of coffee with you," she laugh, and noticed how his eyes lit up. Did he really think she might turn him down?

"Where would you like to go? Are you finished shopping?" he asked, all in one breath, while he got a better grip on a package that was slipping out of his arms.

"Well, not really, but I can finish the rest of my shopping tomorrow," she answered his second question first. "It's almost nine o'clock now. I know of a cute little German coffee shop around the corner from here. Would you like to meet there?"

"Sure, in about fifteen minutes?" he asked, as he hoisted all of his packages once more into a better position to carry.

Maggie laugh again, "Are you sure you can make it to your car?"

"Just be there in fifteen minutes," he hollered as he hurried away to his car.

The German coffee shop was dimly lit without too many customers at this hour. Thick wooden tables and chairs covered the front area, with high backed booths along the back windows giving it an appearance of the Medieval period. A German song ended on the speakers and Silent Night softly filled the almost empty restaurant. The hostess in her long German costume ask if they would prefer a booth.

"Yes, we would. Thank you," answered Jess. "We only want coffee and maybe a dessert this evening," he said, as the hostess started to hand them menus.

"This evening our specialty dessert is Christmas Plum Pudding. We also have our original Black Forrest Cake and several varieties of pies. While you decide I'll inform your waitress that you only want coffee and dessert."

"Thank you," Jess murmured.

"Thank you and have a very nice evening," she said, as she hurried off.

"This is nice, very quaint, don't you think?" Maggie smiled, while looking around at the interior of the restaurant.

"Yes, it's very different. You have a beautiful smile," Jess said, and was silent for awhile, as if he wanted to say more, but was afraid of rushing her. "What are you plans for Christmas?"

"Oh, the usual family get together at our home. We always have Christmas at Rosebriar. Bill's parents and brother and sister and their families will be there, plus my parents and my brother and his family, and of course Julie and her new husband. Jonathan will be home from college. It will be quite a house full."

"Do you have to cook for that many people?" he asked.

"My housekeeper/cook will do most of the cooking, but I'll help with some of my special Christmas receipts."

"And what might that be?"

"Well, I'll probably cook Goose with chestnut and liver stuffing. And a sausage fruit stuffing for the turkey. Maybe for a dessert, souffle-filled crepes with red raspberry sauce."

"Stop! You're making me hungry," Jess told her laughing.

"Now tell me what you're doing for Christmas."

"I wish I was spending it with you," he hesitated, "alone. We'll scratch this year, but next Christmas, watch out."

"Oh, you sound sure of yourself, don't you?"

"Yes, Maggie, I love you. I am crazily and madly in love with you. I don't want just a passing affair. I swear to you I have never had an affair, even after Adrian's accident. I had no desire for anyone until you."

"I believe you, Jess. I wouldn't be here if I didn't think you were honest about this."

"I know you're unhappy too, Maggie. You smile on the outside to cover it up, but I can see the sadness in your eyes. You don't laugh on the inside where it really matters."

"No, I'm not real happy. I've been depressed for the last six months or more. I can't seem to pull myself out of it. I keep thinking I should see a therapist, but then I put it off. I have everything, but yet something is missing. I thought my depression was because I'm going to be forty, but after being with you I know it's more."

Jess took her hands in his and gently raised them to his lips. "I'm very happy when I'm with you. I tried not to love you, Maggie, tried to get you out of my mind so many times. You've even drifted in during some major operations and I've almost made several mistakes on the operating table, but I made you slip out just in time," he softly laugh.

Maggie squeezed his hand, "I do love you too, Jess. I've tried to fight it because of circumstances, but unfortunately it's bigger than my will power." Several buttons of his plaid wool shirt were opened at the top and Maggie had a desire to touch his tanned chest and run her fingers through the dark hair that obviously covered it.

The waitress came to take their order. Maggie had the Christmas Plum Pudding, while Jess tried the Black Forrest Cake. It was hard to even concentrate while being so near him, Maggie thought to herself. She felt like a young school girl having her first crush. But she had feelings inside of a woman, a burning desire to know everything about this man, to share the tenderest and most intimate moments with him. She came back to reality as the waitress returned with their desserts and ask if they needed anything else. After the waitress left Maggie started to say something but hesitated.

"Tell me what you were going to say," Jess teased.

"Jess, there is one favor I've been meaning to ask of you. It has nothing to do with us, and you have to promise complete secrecy," Maggie said with a mysterious note in her voice.

"Well now, if it has nothing to do with us it couldn't be too exciting, but for you," he said slowly, "of course I'll do anything."

"You've probably heard of the Christmas basket given to a needy family in our town," Maggie began, "Well, my family has been doing this for years. It was started by my grandmother. I need to get it delivered to the Julio Martinez family and the person that delivers the basket for me every year is sick for awhile." Maggie looked pleadingly at Jess. "I thought maybe you would deliver it for me since you are traveling all over the area, and tell them it's a gift from someone that thought they could use it."

"So you're the secret Santa that the media gets all excited about. Sure I would be glad to play Santa Clause. I think that giving food and toys to some family at Christmas is wonderful. I mean most of us donate money to an organization, and most of the time we don't even know for sure who that money ends up with, but to go to all the work of shopping for the food and toys and the baking that I hear goes into that basket, I think it's just great."

"Well, I love doing it. Now you haven't told me what you're doing for Christmas yet?"

"We're flying to Arizona to Adrian's brother's home. Our son, Cris, and his wife and two children will be going with us. Some other members of Adrian's family will also be there." He stopped . "I wish it was you I was spending Christmas with," he told her, as they eyes met in a special way that only lovers know. They held hands across the table absorbed in this new excited feeling that was created between them.

"Jess, what are we going to do? We can't just pretend Adrian and Bill doesn't exist."

"I know how you feel, but we're important too, Maggie. We're both unhappy with our marriages. I'd like to get out of my marriage, divorce Adrian, but I can't. She's crippled and I'm the one that caused it. I owe her my life, Maggie, but not my love. I have no desire for her, except to take care of her. I try to make her happy with gifts and vacations, whatever she wants. But my love for her was over a long time before the car accident. We were heading for a divorce then, but we were trying to wait until Cris went away to college. Then after the accident, Adrian clung to me. She was so afraid of being alone and helpless, I couldn't leave her then or now." Jess kept on talking, and Maggie knew he had never told anyone all this before. "No one knows how hard it's been. Adrian has always been spoiled and difficult to live with, even before she was crippled. After the accident she became worse. I suppose that's why I work such long hours, it's a living hell at home."

"I had no idea your life was like this. You always seemed like everything was fine when you were out at the ranch. I just assumed you and Adrian had a good life together, even under the circumstances of her being crippled."

"I have a very hard time keeping nurses and housekeepers for her. She swears at them and throws things at them. She makes unbelievable messes for them to clean up," Jess went on.

"I suppose my situation is similar, Jess. I love Bill, but I'm not in love with him. I have no desire to do things with him, to sleep with him, or anything else that married couples enjoy doing together. We're civil to each other, and I don't think Bill really realizes there is anything wrong with our marriage," Maggie went on "We don't talk about intimate things. He wants sex and I lay there, because—because," she groped for words "he doesn't seem to think I need love or sex."

They were both silent again, just holding hands across the table for a long time. Maggie glanced at her watch. "Oh, it's ten thirty. I better get going. I have an early appointment with a customer tomorrow for a fitting."

"Me too, I have an early surgery schedule."

When they reached Maggie's car in the dimly lit parking area, Jess pulled her into his arms. She didn't resist him as his lips possessed her. She curled her arms around his neck, forgetting their other lives. He touched one of her breast underneath her coat, messaging it gently through her sweater and bra drawing her closer to him. She had to fight the desire and knew it was even harder for Jess.

"I better let you go, Maggie, before it's too late," he whispered. "Please don't make me wait too long. I love you so."

"I feel the same way, Jess, but I have to sort out my feelings, I can't rush into this. All I can tell you now is that I do love you very very much."

"That's all I need to hear. Bye Darling," he said as he kissed her gently and walked toward his own car. "I'll call you before Christmas and pick that basket up to deliver. After this Christmas we're going to spend a lot of holidays together someway."

CHAPTER 3

Maggie looked at her watch again. It was four ten in the late afternoon. The mare had been down in labor for forty minutes. One front foot and the nose had appeared still in the birth sack, and Maggie debated whether or not to break the sack over the foal's nose and head to try to get a better hold of it to pull it out, but she was also afraid if it went back in the birth canal than it could suffocate. She had seen enough foals be born to know that the foal should have passed through the birth canal completely within a matter of minutes once the head appeared.

The dark chestnut quarter mare got up when the foal was not born and nervously circled her stall and lay back down on her other side and strained and pushed to try to born her foal.

"Darn, why did she have to go in labor just when Bill is gone," Maggie said aloud to herself, and pulled her coat up around her neck to keep the chill off on the late winter afternoon.

She picked up the phone in the barn office and dialed the veterinarian's office. "Dr. Morgan, please," said Maggie.

"I'm sorry, Dr. Morgan is out on a call. He's been gone about an hour and should be calling in anytime. His assistant, Dr. Hilford, can take your call," the office lady told her.

"Well, it's an emergency. This is Maggie Lancing. My mare is trying to foal and she's having trouble. But I would rather have Dr. Morgan look at her.

I'll wait for fifteen minutes and if Dr. Morgan hasn't called or got here by then I'll call back. My number is 446-5620."

"Okay, that's Rosebriar Ranch. I'll try to reach him for you."

Maggie returned to the stall. The mare was still down and one leg and the nose of the foal had appeared again. It was hard to tell whether the foal was alive or still born through the placenta. It was so still.

"Oh, please God, let this foal be alive. And please let Dr. Morgan get here soon." Maggie prayed. Maggie prayed a lot. That's why she was so concerned about her feelings for Jess. She knew it was wrong. A sin. Adultery. She prayed for strength in her weakness for him.

The mare gave a low whinny. She was wet with sweat from the pain of trying to born her foal. Maggie patted the mare on her shoulder. "Take it easy, Tiffany, the vet will be here soon."

Maggie knew if Jess got word he would be here as fast as he could. She could always depend on him for emergencies. Dr. Hilford seemed to be a good vet, but he was young with only six months experience behind him.

About ten minutes had passed before Maggie saw headlights speeding up the driveway. Jess jumped out and hurried toward the barn.

"How is the mare, Maggie?" He asked, glancing at the quarter mare.

"She's been up and down for fifty two minutes and one foot and nose keeps appearing. I think the other leg is caught,"

"You're probably right, hold it there, Mama," Jess said to the mare, patting her on the hip. He put his hand inside the mare, gently breaking the placenta. "Now if I can just get a hold of that little leg. I feel it. It's really caught. It's coming down." He drew his hand out. "There Mama, have your baby," he said, smiling.

Maggie felt relieved. Thank you Lord she whispered. Everything would be fine now. At times she had too much confidence in Jess as a doctor. Almost as if he could perform miracles too, after some of the ways he had doctored and done surgery on their animals over the years. Not one of their animals had ever died under his care.

25

The chestnut foal looked around at his new environment and let out a deep low whinny. The mare was too tired to get up yet, but raised her head to look at him. She whinnied back to him and he tried to get up pulling the rest of the placenta off his hips and hind legs.

"Isn't he adorable. Looks just like Mama with that white stripe down his face," Maggie said, as she and Jess watched, letting nature take its course from here on.

"All babies are adorable, Maggie. Have you got the iodine ready?" Jess asked.

The foal stood up then, and the umbilical cord broke. Maggie knew it should always break naturally unless there was some problem, because as much blood as possible should drain from the umbilical cord into the foal's body. Jess put the iodine on the navel while Maggie helped him hold the foal, than she grabbed a clean terry cloth towel that she had brought out from the house and started drying him.

"Well, we will have to find name for you little fellow. And with your bloodlines it will have to be a good one," Maggie laugh and kissed him on his wet nose.

Tiffany got up, dropping her afterbirth as she did. Jess took the placenta out of the stall with a pitch fork and inspected it carefully.

"Looks like it's all here, what should I do with it?" he asked

"Put in that wheelbarrow for now, and Bill can bury it later," she answered.

"Do you want me to give them their shots, Maggie?"

"As long as you're already here, Jess, I would appreciate it if you would."

The chill in the air became colder as it turned dusk. The beauty of the sky stood out as the sun started setting, leaving a bright pink sunset in the west. Maggie had not seen Jess since before Christmas, almost two months ago, but he had called her every week on the phone. They were both so busy that the time passed quickly and it was already the end of February.

"It's cold out here. How about a cup of hot coffee or tea before you go?" She asked, as she held the mare while Jess gave her two shots in the hip.

"You're alone Maggie?" Jess asked.

"Yes. Oh come on, Jess, we're adults, we can control our emotions."

Jess hesitated for a moment. "I better not, Maggie, I have several more calls to make yet this evening."

They both stood looking at each other for what seemed a long time, then Jess extended his hand out to Maggie. She slowly put her hand in his and he drew her close.

"I love you so," he told her.

"I love you too, Jess, but I wish I didn't, it's so wrong."

"I know it's wrong, but what I feel for you is beautiful." He just held her close for awhile. "I have to go to a seminar in San Francisco in several weeks. Meet me there, Maggie, Please."

Maggie was silent as she looked deep into Jess's gray-blue eyes while they pleated for an answer of yes. "I'll meet you there," she finally said.

Maggie unlocked the hotel door. The clerk at the desk had looked at her with what she thought was suspicion, when he raised an eyebrow, as she asked for a message from Jess and number to his room. There was a message that he had left the key at the desk for her.

The large room was beautifully decorated in yellow, pale green and beige. A large window over looked the bay and beyond that Maggie could see the ocean stretched out for miles. In the other direction all one could see was skyscraper after skyscraper. She could only imagine the beauty of the lights at night. A king size bed was at one end of the room with a bright yellow flower print bedspread covering it. A beige and yellow flowered sofa with end tables and a coffee table was at the other end of the room. A large vase of yellow flowers with baby breath graced the coffee table.

A piece of paper with "Maggie" written on the outside was propped up on the dresser by the bed, as though the author wanted to be sure to attract her attention to it. Maggie opened it with trembling hands.

My Dearest Maggie,

If you really come to me, you'll never know how happy it will make me. Your love has given me something to live for. I only wish we could be together forever as man and wife.

Love, Jess

Maggie shivered as a sensation rushed through her. The thought of being completely Jess's tonight, body and soul, was overwhelming. She had wanted this since last fall. Now the time finally was here and she was nervous and scared. But the need to love and be loved by him prevailed over anything else. She opened her suitcase taking some of the clothes out. He's so romantic so unlike Bill she thought. She reminded herself that she wasn't going to think about Bill tonight, or Jess's wife and spoil these two beautiful days. For one night and a day only she and Jess would exist. She finished unpacking and hung her things in the closet. The lock on the door clicked and Jess opened the door. He smiled at her and she saw a relieved look cross his face.

"You really came," he said as he pulled her into his arms.

"Didn't you think I would, Jess.?"

"Well," he hesitated, "I know you love me, but your morals are kind of high. I thought at the last minute you might back out."

"Well, I didn't. I'm really here," she laugh.

He drew her closer, kissing her lightly on the lips a few times before crushing her to him. The long awaited desire swept through Maggie and a guarantee of the one precious night and day that lay ahead.

Jess gently let her go, "would you like to go to the dining room for dinner? I hear the food here is pretty good."

She sensed his awkwardness at being alone with her here. "Sure, I'm kind of hungry after that long drive here. I'll just check my makeup and grab a jacket."

After dinner they had another glass of wine and danced for awhile. Maggie felt that Jess was trying not to rush her back to the hotel room, but dancing close to him was almost unbearable, and she wondered why he felt he should keep prolonging the evening down here in the cocktail lounge.

She leaned back slightly looking up at him. He was only about two inches taller than she was. Just right for dancing together, and he was a great dancer. He whispered something in her ear, but the band was playing a loud song and Maggie could not understand him. She tried to relax in his arms, but her thoughts drifted to the evening ahead. She wished she could stay in his arms forever. But he was all hers tonight. Unfortunately, they would have to go their own way when they returned to Wilcottville. But she would have this memory to take with her, to live on until they could be together again.

She knew she should feel more guilty than she did, deceiving Bill and loving another women's husband, but she again vowed to forget about them tonight. She closed her eyes and lightly kissed Jess on the neck.

He held her closer. "Let's get out of here," he whispered. The elevator going up to the room was empty except for them. Jess smiled shyly at her and took her hand. "Are you sorry you came?" He asked.

"No, no, crazy maybe, but not sorry," she smiled. Her face softened. "I'm scared, Jess. I've never been with anyone except Bill, " she added.

He pulled her gently to him, "I would never hurt you in anyway, believe me Darling. Tonight only we exist. We have no marital partner, no children, no jobs, nothing. We are on this planet entirely alone."

Jess unlocked the door to their room and swooped Maggie up, carrying her to the bed where he gently sat her down. He slowly undressed her and she him. There was no need to talk. They had been talking for months and now the need to have each other completely was so great that nothing else mattered.

He massaged her breasts while he moved his lips from hers, slowly kissing her neck moving down to her breast before he hungrily placed his mouth over her taut nipple while she moaned with pleasure.

"My darling, Maggie, I've never known anyone like you before. You're kind and gentle and loving. You're always thinking of others before yourself."

"Jess, just love me, so our real world will disappear. I need you," she whispered, as she arched her body to his, pulling his head down to meet her lips.

He moaned, and she knew he liked her aggressivenes, as the San Francisco lights danced through their tenth story window, enclosing them in their own magical world of shining lights and dancing rainbows.

Maggie woke up early the next morning with the sun shining brightly into the room. She turned over in bed and Jess was there. The memory of last night sent a lovely chill through her. How nice to wake up with him beside her. She reached over and gently touched his ear, than kissed it. Jess quickly grabbed her, laughing.

"Silly, I thought you were asleep," she said.

"Well, I was, but I like the way you woke me," he answered, as he rolled her up on top of him. "Are you tired today, after frolicking with an old doctor all night, Miss Maggie?"

"Um----- I'm worn out, but it's a good worn out feeling," she laughed. "And you're not old, we're not old. Life doesn't begin until forty I heard. In fact doctor, you've never told me how old you are." She became serious, "Jess, there are so many things I don't know about you."

"Well, Ma Lady, just what would you like to know?"

"Well, let's start with your age. How old are you?" she asked teasingly.

"I'm forty four, and my birthday is on July 21st. Now don't forget that date."

"Oh, you're a Leo. Leo's have very good qualities."

"Well, that's one thing in my favor," Jess added.

He looked seriously into her deep blue eyes before he brought her lips down to meet his. She could feel his passion mounting and his bear body next to hers became tense. He was gentle and patient. She had never known this feeling of being able to say words of love openly before, to touch and caress until they were both lost in a diminutive world beyond return.

"I don't have to be at the seminar until three o'clock today, would you like to do some sightseeing and then have a crab and lobster lunch," asked Jess.

"Sounds great, and then I'll have to visit a couple of my customers here before I head back home," answered Maggie.

They walked through several shops and bought a few souvenirs to take home before they found a seafood restaurant with a fabulous view overlooking the bay and miles of ocean. Several sailboats were in view which added to the picturesque setting.

Jess took Maggie's hand in his after they sat down at the table the waiter had taken them to. "Darling, you'll never know how happy you've made me. I couldn't bear the thought of losing you now that I finally have you."

She smiled at him, "Jess, I've never had feelings like this before. I feel like I've never really loved anyone before you. Just looking at you now sends feelings through me that, well, It's sinful, Jess, what you do to me."

After lunch they walked along the pier watching the boats and Sea Gulls. The ocean smell was an over powering mixture of sea life, vegetation and a sharp crispness of fresh ocean air blowing in their faces. The waves pounded the rocks below and the Sea Gulls called out to each other in an unforgettable sound.

"Maggie, we won't be able to see each other for awhile," Jess said, as he turned toward her and pulled her hair back in a gesture of love. Leaning toward her he kissed her on the nose.

She took him by the hand kissing the back of it as they continued walking. "Maybe it's best if we just see each other several times a year," she told him.

"I was hoping we could manage to get together every other month somewhere," he stated.

"There's so many problems. What if we run into someone we know. What will we do, Jess, if Bill or Adrian find out? I don't know how I'm going to face Bill when I get back. I know I have guilt written all over me. And we're sinning, Jess, this is adultery."

"I'm so sorry of putting you through this, Maggie. I wish there was some other way. Remember I love you and it will workout for us someday to be together always."

"Well, if we're never together again, Jess, we have this one beautiful night and day to remember. I know it's wrong, but I will always cherish this time with you."

"Thank you, Darling, for coming here. I couldn't have went on much longer without making love to you," he teased, and put his arm around her shoulders pulling her close to him as they walked down the old cracked sidewalk toward his car.

"Maggie, we'll have to take one day at a time. I don't know what's going to happen in the future, but—," he stopped walking and pulled her around to face him, "I'm going to look forward to spending the rest of my life with you, someday as my wife. I don't know how yet, but it will work out. We have to have faith in this."

"I want that to, Jess, but as the situation now stands, you can't leave Adrian while she's so dependent on you, and I couldn't ask Bill to leave when he's worked so hard his whole life developing our land and raising the cattle. It would kill him. I could never sell Rosebriar, the home my grandparents built to split everything with Bill."

"Well, let's not do anything rational. This will work out for us, Maggie. We just have to be patient, and take each day at a time. You're not an impatient person, are you? I've seen you wait weeks for those overdue mares to foal. And the way you patiently care for a sick baby calf. And what about the time your dog was ran over and had a broken leg? You carried that dog from the house to outside and back for weeks until he could walk again."

Maggie giggled, "You noticed all that? I thought you were so busy that you never looked at me. All you ever talked about was the animals. I thought that was all you were interested in."

"Hey Lady, you caught my eye a long time ago."

"How long ago?" Maggie asked.

"Well, let's see," he slowly said, "I've always thought you were very beautiful and kind," he stopped for a few seconds. "And so gentle with your animals.

You reminded me of a little girl at times, and I guess I just gradually fall in love with you. Now when did you first notice me?" He asked boldly.

"Well, I thought you were so good looking. And I knew Adrian was paralyzed and I wondered how does a man like you cope without sex. I imagined all the lonely ranch wives where you went were probably after you, right?"

" A few. You can't imagine some of the excuses they used to try to get me into their house. But I knew their intentions and avoided the crises without being too unkind and without losing customers I hope."

"And you were always innocent?" Maggie asked mischievously.

"Always, until you. You captured my heart and I couldn't help falling in love with you," he teased back.

CHAPTER 4

Maggie pulled her western boots on with the anticipation of riding Tiffany today. The mare and colt had been stalled since he was born, with only their paddock to exercise in and they needed the freedom badly.

She had given Alice and Jennifer, and also her housekeeper the day off, and wanted to just relax at home by herself. Bill would be gone the whole day branding the new calves and the banding the little bulls in one of the pastures.

"Easy Mama, your baby is okay. He's just getting some exercise," Maggie consoled the mare while leading her out of the stall, and the little colt ran around them feeling good to be free of fences. She tied the mare at the hitching post where she had put her saddle and blanket on the ground beside it. She brushed the mare, untangling a matted piece of her mane before she attempted to saddle her.

Maggie looked up as an old car drove up the driveway and stopped about thirty feet from where Maggie was grooming the mare. Julio Martinez got out.

"Ah—Miss Maggie, you're going riding today," he said in his Spanish accent.

"Yes, Julio, what can I do for you?"

"Is Mr. Bill at home?"

"No, he's out branding the calves today."

"Are you all alone?" he asked, "I don't see any other cars around today, so you must be alone."

Maggie stopped brushing the mare and looked up at him. His voice sounded different and she saw a grimace cross his face and a strange look in his dark angry eyes. He wore a knife in a holster attached to his belt and put his hand on it as he moved toward her. Maggie started backing away, but he lunged at her, grabbing her by the wrist while she screamed and tried to hit him with the horse brush still in her other hand. The mare panic, pulling back against the nylon halter and heavy rope which held her steadfast, while the colt ran wildly around her, Maggie and her assailant.

"I knew Mr. Bill would be gone today branding the calves and hoped you would be alone," he laugh, showing his brown tobacco stained teeth, as he pushed her toward the barn.

"Julio, wait, wait, what are you doing?" Maggie screamed.

He laugh again. "I'm revenging your husband for firing me twice. Nobody fires Julio Martinez and gets away with it. Even though he won't know that I raped his beautiful wife, because you won't tell him or go to the Sheriffs, because if you do I promise you I will then seek out and rape your beautiful daughter, Julie. Ah! That would be a pleasure, that young tender body," he laugh.

Maggie kicked at him and struggled to pull lose, but he was so much bigger and stronger it was like an elf fighting a giant.

"Julio, I'll talk to Bill and beg him to rehire you," she promised. Please don't do this. You're drunk. I can smell the liquor on you. Please don't. You'll be sorry tomorrow when you get sober."

He kept pulling her toward the barn while she fought and kicked him. "So, we have a little tiger here, all the more exciting, Miss Maggie," he said, as he grabbed her around the waist with one of his huge arms pulling her back side against him and twisting one of her arms behind her. Shoving her to the hard barn floor, he lunged on top of her pulling at her jeans and ripping her shirt.

"No, please don't, please don't," she screamed.

"Shut up you woman slut," he hollered. "All women are sluts, you included."

Maggie opened her eyes and saw the wild look on his face as he was still pulling at her jeans and blouse. His sweaty odor and liquor breath gagged her and she thought she was going to vomit. She heard the mare and colt running around the yard and knew the mare must have broken loose. She hoped they would not leave the yard and venture down the driveway onto the road.

In one last attempt she doubled her free fist and punched Julio as hard as she could. It seemed as though her assailant hardly felt it and slapped her hard across the face. She screamed again.

"Nobody can hear you little woman. Shut up or do you want me to use my knife on you?" he hollered as he again struck her across the face and grabbed a hand full of her hair banging her head against the hard floor. Everything went black for Maggie.

When she came to her body and head ached. Her clothes were half torn off her. She sat up and looked around for any sign of Julio before getting to her feet and pulling her clothes on.

The horses, the mare and colt were still loose she remembered, while her head pounded. No sign of Julio or his car were seen. She saw the mare standing by the back fence, but didn't see the colt at first, until she got closer and saw he was caught in the barbed wire fence.

The mare whinnied to her as Maggie whirled and ran to the barn to get the wire cutters, forgetting her own aches and pains.

"Oh God, please don't let him be cut up." She knew how dangerous barbed wire was when a horse is caught and struggles to get loose. The harder they fight the more entwined they become and deeper the cuts. She raced back to the mare and colt stopping far enough back not to frightened the foal, "easy little guy," she gently said as she slowly moved toward him. He started to struggle again but then lay quiet as if he knew Maggie would get him out of his terrible predicament.

She cut the two wires that held him prisoner, and saw he had a large gash on his shoulder that would have to be sutured and a small one on his front leg. The rest of the dozen or so cuts were small or only scratches.

"You're a lucky little fellow that you were not cut real bad," Maggie told him , as she rubbed his neck and he whinnied to his mother. "Well, let's get you back into your stall and I'll call the vet to sew up these cuts."

Maggie asked for either of the veterinarians to come out, because she didn't particularly want to see Jess right now and hoped he wouldn't get the call. She longed to lay in a nice hot bath, and wash the terrible uncleanliness away, but she had to settle for a fast shower before the vet arrived. About twenty minutes later she heard the truck drive up and saw Jess going into the barn. By the time she got to the barn he was coming back to his truck to get the shots and utensils he needed.

"Hi, Maggie, I see the colt's cut up. How did that happen?"

"Something frightened the mare and she broke loose from the hitching post," she answered, hoping he wouldn't ask anymore about it.

"Well, that one cut is kind of deep, but I think it will heal okay. It could be worse. Barbed wire wasn't it?"

Jess tranquilized the colt and waited for the drug to take effect before he started suturing him. "What have you been doing, Maggie?" He asked with concern in his voice.

"Keeping busy with the leather business. I've started looking for a building in town," she answered.

"Sounds like business is really good."

"Yes, I need to hire two more employees and I suppose an agent to take care of the out of town sales. I just don't have the time to do all the traveling anymore," she said, as she rubbed her forehead trying to make the pain go away.

"Do you have a headache, Maggie?"

"Yes, I have a slight one." She couldn't tell Jess how bad her head and face really did hurt or he may suspect something..

"Here let me message your head and neck for you," Jess said as moved closer. "Why is your face so red and kind of puffy on one side?"

"Oh, I must have hit it when the mare broke loose," she said—hating to lie to Jess, but she couldn't tell him that Julio raped her, not yet anyway. He may want to call the Sheriff's and she had to sort this out. She couldn't endanger her daughter's life, and she knew Julio would go through with the threat or send someone else to do it if he couldn't. No, she had to think things out. She wasn't hurt, just shaken up, and she couldn't tell anyone yet, not even Jess.

"Well, an ice pack would help," Jess consoled her, as he finished messaging her and kissed her lightly on the neck before he walked to his truck and gathered the instruments needed from the isolated unit to suture the colt.

"Do you think you can hang onto him while I stitch him up?" He asked, "I know you don't feel good and I suggest you go lay down and take a nap when I leave, but I do need your help for awhile."

"Jess, I'm okay, I can hold the colt." The colt was groggy and it didn't take too much effort to hold him. In fact, he kept trying to fall asleep standing up and Maggie would have to rub him on the neck and head to keep him from falling. He hardly felt the needle going in and out through his skin, and their quiet conversation seemed to soothe him.

After Jess put the colt back in the stall he looked at his watch, "I'm over an hour late on a ranch call, so I have to run. But I miss you, Maggie. Thank heavens for the telephone or I would be going crazy not knowing what you are doing. At least we can keep in touch. But one question, am I calling you at the right time? I know you're busy too."

"Jess, I'm happy to hear from you anytime. I know you don't have much time. Bill never answers my shop phone, so keep calling there."

Jess pulled her into his arms, "I'm sorry you don't feel good."

Tears welled up in her eyes. She chocked, "Just tell me that you still love me."

"Hey Darling, what's wrong?" He asked, "Of course I still love you. I'll always love you. Don't ever doubt that." He kissed her on the lips, not passionately, but with so much love that Maggie felt her heart would bust with her love for this man who had so much feeling and concern for her. She felt fortunate to have his love even if it was second hand. He always seemed concern about other people too, and especially for the animals he doctored. Maggie could not think of another person she knew with a heart as big as his.

With a soft cry, she wrapped her arms around him clinging to him. His hands rubbed her neck and back gently coaxing the taut muscles to relax. She felt safe and comfortable, safe from Julio. In Jess's arms the rape seemed like only a bad dream. She would like to stay here forever, but she knew she had to let him go to his already late appointment.

"Thank you, for being you and for loving me. Please go. I'm okay and you're really late now. Bye," she said and ran toward the house turning to wave as Jess's truck pulled away.

Maggie ran up the stairs and flung herself across her bed. She had to get her thoughts together and try to figure out what she should do about Julio. How could he do this to her. She always thought of his family as friends, even though she didn't know them very well, they always spoke and carried on small conversations. And she had sent his family the Christmas basket. She realized Julio and his family didn't know where the basket came from, but how could he be that vengeful as to hurt her—to rape her. Thank Heavens she couldn't get pregnant. That was one thing she didn't have to worry about, but what if he had a disease. She couldn't report it. She would have to go to the Sheriff's Department if she did and they would question her and then it would be in the newspapers. In a small town like Wilcottville everyone would know. He could get to Julie before he was arrested or send someone else after her. These thoughts went over and over in Maggie's mind until she drifted off into a deep sleep where Julio and the other farm workers were all chasing her, but she couldn't find a hiding place and kept running and running.

She woke up in a sudden start and her body shook as the memory of being raped returned to her-----"No, it didn't happen, it didn't," she cried, but she realized it really did happen. She ran a hot tub of water and soaked in it trying to wash some of the bad memory away. She knew she wouldn't report it out of fear for Julie and the publicity it could cause. She had to worn Julie someway without letting her know the truth.

CHAPTER 5

The next morning Maggie's head felt better, and the red puffiness was not too noticeable. She had not seen Bill last night, as he had come home after dark, and Maggie had taken some sleeping pills after her hot bath and went to bed early in her bedroom. She heard him talking to Zelma, as she was coming in and he was leaving at daybreak.

Maggie pulled herself out of bed, wishing she could soak in the hot tub again and then go back to bed, but she had a dozen things that had to be done today. She had to do a fitting on a customer at eight o'clock, then unpack some leather supplies that arrived three days ago. At noon she had a luncheon in Sacramento with a new client to sign the final papers to carry her line of leather clothing and accessories. She had been excited about Roby International buying her line, because they were very exclusive and expensive, with stores nation wide and in some major overseas countries. But today, after what happened yesterday, it seemed of less significance.

She looked at herself in the dresser mirror. "I can't go to that luncheon looking like this," she said aloud , as she flipped the back part of her long dark blond hair up on her head and closely examined her slightly puffy face.. The ice packs had helped yesterday, but it still looked awful. She decided she would leave the unpacking go until tomorrow and make an appointment for a facial, a manicure, and her hair to be shampooed and styled.

She called the beauty shop that she sometimes went to and they were able to work her in early enough to have her finished by eleven o'clock. Julie, she had to call Julie right away, to meet her and warn her someway about Julio without her being suspicious.

"Hello."

"Julie, this is mother. How are you and Steve?"

"We're fine, Mother, how are you and dad?"

"We're doing okay, Julie, but I miss you and would like to talk to you."

"Well, I have classes all week."

"What time is your last class over today?"

"At three O'clock," Julie answered.

"Good. Could you meet me right after three in Sacramento?"

"Sure. I take it you have business in Sacramento today?"

"Yes, I'm signing the final papers with Roby International."

"Oh, Mom, that's great. Coming up in the world, aren't you?" Julie laugh.

"Darling, I have to run now. I'm getting the works at Beauty Flair."

"Oh, I can't wait to see you," she said excitedly, "Bye Mother, see you by three thirty. Oh, where will we meet?"

"How about that little coffee shop about three blocks south of your campus, what's it called?"

"Oh, you mean the Coffee House. Okay, see you there. Bye now."

"Julie, please be careful."

"Mother, is something wrong? You sound so down today. Not excited like you should be on a historical day of signing with Roby International."

Maggie laugh softly. Her daughter had always known her like a book. She always sensed her moods and inner feelings.

"Everything is fine. I just need to talk to you."

41

The day was going well. The beautician even finished with Maggie ten minutes early. The lunch business meeting with Rodger Baysinger, the executive with Roby International, had been successful with everything signed. She was at the Coffee House waiting for Julie. She was about twenty minutes early, but this would give her some time to think of what she should tell Julie to warn her about Julio. She sipped her hot coffee and racked her mind trying to come up with a solution so that Julie would not become apprehensive or suspicious.

Maggie looked at herself in the wall mirror by the booth she was sitting in. She had always liked her hair on top of her head with a few curls circling the crown. The makeup artist had applied more makeup than Maggie usually wore, and the dark blue shadow made her large eyes look even bluer. She had noticed earlier when she walked up to the table where Mr. Baysinger was waiting for her, that his eyes widened in pleasure, and a smile crossed his face as he stood up moving his eyes down her slender body. She wore a light summer suit of a navy blue jacket with small white stripes and navy skirt. Her navy and white heels matched perfectly. Mr. Baysinger had hinted about their getting together very soon, but Maggie had evaded the subject until he finally took the hint that she was not interested in anything but a business relationship.

She saw Julie come into the coffee House and her thoughts returned to Julio and fear for Julie.

"Hi, Mother," she said, and kissed Maggie on the cheek. "You look fantastic. You always look great though. I hope I look as good as you at forty."

"Forty isn't so bad after all. You make me sound like I'm ancient," she laugh.

Julie slumped into the booth. "All these final exams are wearing me out. I stayed up until one thirty a.m. studying for this exam I had today, and it was so hard, I don't even know if I passed it."

"Of course you will. You're very intelligent," Maggie assured her.

The waitress came up to their table and Julie ordered a coke and a muffin. "Now Mother, what is this all important matter that you need to talk to me about."

A concerned look crossed Maggie's face, "Darling, I'm worried," she hesitated for a moment. "Julio has been acting strange. You know your father fired him last fall, and he came out to the ranch the other day, he was drinking, and he threatened to get revenge. Your dad wasn't there."

"Revenge. Because he goofed up with his drinking and got fired? Oh, Mother, he was probably just talking. What did Dad say?" Julie looked squarely at her. "You did tell Dad, didn't you?"

"No, no, you know how mad your father would get, and it would just cause more trouble. Julio was drunk and maybe didn't know all he was talking about, but Julie, he mentioned rape and I just wanted to warn you to be careful. Keep your doors locked and don't go out alone at night."

"Mother, what did he say? Did he try to hurt you?"

"No, no, Julie," she hoped her daughter couldn't grasp her inter most feelings now. "I couldn't understand him too well, but he frightened me and I'm afraid he may carry out his intentions."

"Maybe we should go to the Sheriffs," Julie now sounded worried.

"No," Maggie answered almost too quickly, "They won't do anything on just a threat. Just be careful. I'm sure he doesn't know where you live or would even come to Sacramento. But keep your doors locked and be careful coming and going from your car to your apartment."

"Well, you be careful too and keep your doors locked. Maybe you should get a good watch dog. Sissy and Boy aren't very protective."

"I'll think about that. I'm hardly ever alone though. Usually Zelma or my employees are there. Well, Darling, it's almost five o'clock and I know you have to go home and cook Steve dinner, so I think we should be going."

"Lucky you. You have a cook and housekeeper."

"Well someday when you have a career, you can too. But right now enjoy cooking for Steve and keeping house. I hope later on after you finish college, that you'll come into the clothing business with me. But first finish college and maybe work for awhile in your career before you make a decision."

"You're advice sounds pretty good and your offer, but it seems so far away. I wish I was through college."

Maggie brushed her daughter's hair back from her face. "Your college years are some of the most happiest of your life, Julie, don't rush them. Don't rush your life like I've always done. Relax and enjoy these years. Someday you'll look back and see how important and happy these years are."

"You and Dad have never been really happy together, have you?" She asked, without waiting for an answer. "I hope someday you"ll both find happiness. Even if it's with somebody else."

Maggie was shocked that Julie knew she and Bill were never really happy with each other. And more surprised that she would even say anything. Did she suspect something?

"I think your Dad is happy and content with his life, and I'm content with mine."

"Mom, I'm proud of you. From a house and farm wife to a clothing empire with Roby International." They both busted out laughing. "How are you going to do it all?"

"With a bigger shop and more employees," answered Maggie, still laughing. "You'll see, it will all work out in time."

They walked out to the parking lot together. "It was so good to see you, Julie. I miss you so much," Maggie said, as she hugged her. "Give Steve my love."

"I really miss you and Dad too. Steve and I are very happy though and everything is going fine. Tell Dad I love him."

On the long drive home Maggie thought of all that had happened over the last few months. Where her life was going she really had no idea, except for the fact that her business would grow larger. She wished she could be with Jess more, but that was almost impossible. A secret love. That's what they had, and nobody else in the world knew about it yet. She felt so guilty, and sorry for Adrian and Bill. She didn't want to love Jess, but she did. And she didn't want to give up this happiness with him. If she had to give him up she felt like she would just wither and die. She was content before, even though she was depressed and dissatisfied with part of her life, she could have kept going.

She decided the only thing she could do was take one day at a time. She prayed that God would help her and give her strength to do the right thing. Her will power was weak when it came to loving Jess. She prayed for Julio, that the Lord would help him too, and protect her family from him. She knew Julio's wife, Angilina. She was about the same age as Maggie with a very sweet personality. Too good for Julio with his temper and his alcohol addiction.

Her thoughts went to Adrian. What would Adrian do if she found out about them. She really did feel sorry for Adrian. It would be terrible to be paralyzed and then to find out your husband was in love with another woman. It would almost kill Adrian she was afraid. She didn't want this on her conscience, but she couldn't quit loving Jess. What's the old saying, 'all's fair in love and war', but she knew it really wasn't, there's honor and integrity.

Maggie pulled into her long driveway. It wasn't quite dark yet and Tiffany and her colt ran to the fence along the front pasture when they saw her car. The tall Blue Spruce trees lined the driveway and the climbing roses along the wooded rail fence was leafed out and starting to bud. They were beautiful all summer and into fall with their dark red blooms stretching along the wood fence. The ranch was named after the roses, 'Rosebriar'. A name chosen by her grandparents many years ago. It was almost like her's and Jess' romance, the sweet smell and beauty of the rose, but they had the problems of the thorns.

Bill was home when she returned, and they sat down to dinner together that Zelma had cooked. He mentioned that he had a Farm Bureau meeting that he had to attend tonight. "I just returned from Sacramento. I signed with Roby International today," Maggie told him before she took a bite of her salad.

"I suppose that you're going to be busier than ever now," Bill answered, "I just don't know how you're going to keep up making all those clothes."

"It will be hard until I can find a building and hire more employees. But it will all work out."

"Well, it's your thing. I know you can do it. You've always done everything you've ever set your mind too," he smiled. "Guess I won't see much of you after you move your shop into town though."

"You'll be so busy this summer anyway, Bill, you won't even miss me."

"Yeah, I have got a lot to do this year. Guess we'll both keep busy," he answered, and picked the newspaper up to glance at the animal market prices and the Stock Market.

CHAPTER 6

The old shop door creaked as Maggie opened it and stepped inside. The musty odor encircled her, but she immediately swept it aside and visualized how she would decorate her new shop and use a lot of potpourri and Lysol to get rid of the bad odor. This was the only shop available in Wilcottville that was large enough to suit her needs. It also had two large glass show cases that was included in the rental price.

She glanced around the room at the stained bare walls, and knew she would paper part of it with a light flowered wall paper, using a very large border to match in soft colors of blues, mauve, and beige. Something romantic had to be added she mused. Lace and ivy on white lattice work frames would work beautifully she decided. She walked to the large back area where eight sewing machines would soon be busily humming away. There was also plenty of room there for inventory and storage, plus a small enclosed office area.

For some reason she had an urgent need to call Jess, to tell him about the shop and her plans for decorating it. They had not been together since San Francisco, except for seeing each other several times when he was doctoring an animal at Rosebriar. She missed him so much, but maybe it was a blessing that they both had such busy careers that couldn't allow them to be together more. At least Maggie knew he loved her and nothing could deny what they felt for each other. There was always hope of being together soon.

She picked up the old black desk phone, thinking it was probably disconnected, but a buzz hummed loudly in her ear. She dialed the clinic number and made a mental note to order a pink telephone.

"Wilcottville Veterinary Clinic," the voice on the other end answered.

"This is Maggie Lansing. May I please speak to Dr. Morgan if he's in?"

"Is this an emergency?" The office voice asked.

"No," answered Maggie, recalling that they had a new employee that did not know her.

"Can you tell me the nature of your call?"

"I just want to speak to Dr. Morgan about something personal," Maggie told her, feeling foolish that she had said personal.

"Well, hold on a moment. I'll have to see if I can reach him for you."

Several minutes passed and Maggie had second thoughts about whether she should have made this call to his office. He was probably very busy and there was the possibility of someone listening on the office line.

"Maggie."

"Jess, hello."

"Maggie, this is a surprise. You hardly ever call me. Is something wrong?"

"No, I just wanted to tell you about the shop I leased. Are you too busy right now to talk? You can call me later. I probably shouldn't have called, it sounds like you are busy."

"No, I always have time to talk to you," Jess reassured her. "Now where is this shop?"

"Right down town on Elm Street. I'm talking on a phone from there now. For some reason the phone wasn't disconnected. The building is big, Jess, I'll have plenty of room here for everything. I can hire more employees, buy more sewing machines and really get into production. I have a little office where I'll spend a lot of my time designing patterns."

"Darling, that sounds great. I'm so happy for you. I haven't heard you this excited about something for a long time."

"Well, I can't wait to start cleaning and decorating it. It's a terrible mess now."

"Hey, I have a slow afternoon. Can I come and see the shop?" he asked, "I could be there in half an hour."

"Sure, Jess, I'm going to start cleaning it now, so I'll be here for awhile. The address is 1320 West Elm. Come to the back entrance and knock," she told him.

Maggie unlocked the back door when she heard Jess' knock, and he handed her a small bouquet of Daisies, Carnations and Baby Breath, and pulled a bottle of champagne out of a brown paper bag along with some Brie cheese and sesame crackers.

"Jess, how did you have time to get all this?" she laugh.

"Oh, I'm fast sometimes. Now, we're going to celebrate your new shop."

"Well, let me take you on the grand tour first. It's a little dull now, but just wait until I'm finished with it, you won't know it's the same place," she went on while Jess glanced around.

"Yeah, it's a little plain. It doesn't look like it's been used for awhile. But I know how talented you are, and have the utmost confidence that you will transform this plain ugly old building into a beautiful palace," he teased, while he pulled Maggie into his arms. "I've missed you so," he told her.

"Oh Jess, I've missed you too. It's so lonely not being able to see you and have your arms around me."

He kissed her gently before he crushed her against him. She loved him before, but it was nothing compared to the way she felt about him now. The long months in between of waiting to be with him again strengthened her love for him. Their bodies melted together and she had to have him at any cost, even in this musty dirty old shop.

Jess released her, "Maggie this is no place to make love to you, let's go to a motel out of town."

"No, let's not leave," she said and hesitated. "Wait a minute, I saw some big cushions on a bench in the office." She rushed off to get them. "A little dusty maybe, but they're soft," she said, as she pounded one with her fist to shake off the dust, and than the other one before throwing them down on the shabby old carpet in the back room.

"Do you know you're beautiful, lady, with your hair all messed up and a smudge of dirt on your nose," Jess playfully told her.

She smiled as she opened the paper cups which Jess also thought to buy, while he popped the cork off the champagne bottle, spraying a small amount over them.

"To your new shop," Jess toasted, holding his cup to hers.

"To my someday beautiful shop. You won't recognize it in two weeks, Jess."

"Now do you want some cheese and crackers or do you want to make love, Lady?"

"Jess, I've dreamed every day and night of making love to you again, ever since we left San Francisco."

"I know, I have too, Maggie," he said, as he unbuttoned her blouse. "It's knowing you're so close, within several miles from me, and I can't hold you anytime I want." He took the pins out of her hair letting it fall loosely to her shoulders.

"You have perfect breasts," he told her, as he fondled them and placed his mouth over one. She felt his tongue circle her nipple and her desire soared until she didn't think she could stand another minute without completely having him. Her well manicured finger nail traced the hairline of his forehead before she bent over and nibbled his ear and he groaned with pleasure. "Jess, I need you so," she moaned. They hurriedly undressed each other, practically ripping them off in their desire to consume this fire raging inside, searching for the fulfillment only they could bring to each other.

Afterwards they lay still in each other's arms, as their breathing returned to normal. Still undressed with just a couple pieces of their clothing thrown over them, they had their cheese and crackers and finished their glass of champagne.

"Oh, this is Heaven!" exclaimed Maggie, "Even if it's in this dirty, musty old building, it's Heaven being with you."

"Someday, Maggie, I want to take you everywhere. To Paris, Rome, England. Have you ever been there?"

"No, I haven't. I would love it. Bill is not the traveling type, and we've both been so busy all our lives, we haven't had time to travel."

"We have an appointment to go to those places together before we're too old," he laugh.

"Have you taken Adrian there?"

"Several years after the accident we flew over to England and then went on to France. The country is beautiful. But it was tiring for Adrian and we couldn't do too much sight seeing with her in a wheelchair."

They were both quiet for awhile

" Oh, Maggie, what I would give if that car accident had never happened. Adrian would be whole and I could get a divorce."

"Everything happens for a reason, even though we don't understand. I wish too it could be different. I feel so guilty that I love you. You're Adrian's husband, even if it's in name only. And Bill is so trusting and I'm deceiving him."

All of a sudden Jess asked, "Do you have sex with Bill?"

Maggie hesitated before she answered. "He comes to my room once in awhile. I can't respond because there is no feeling there, but he doesn't seem to care. He only wants his own satisfaction met. So many times I wished that I could shove a book about sex under his nose and he would read it. Please Jess, let's drop this subject. I can't talk about it."

"Even if he is your husband, I can't stand the thought of him having you. Of your naked body next to his. I like Bill, I always have, but it's so different now that I love you."

"Jess, let's get off this subject, please."

"I'm sorry. I just can't help being jealous at times."

He pulled her back laying her head against the pillow. He smothered her face and neck in kisses until she responded and they both forgot Adrain and Bill. This time they were both more relaxed and not so demanding and hurried, as the late afternoon turned dusk in the old building.

The next weeks were very busy for Maggie. She hired some painters to paint the inside of the shop and did the wall papering herself along with some help from Alice and Jennifer. A plush dusty rose carpet was laid in the front shop area and a medium brown in the back room and office. Five new sewing machines were ordered and the three almost new machines that they had been using were moved to the new shop. Alice and Jennifer wanted to use the ones they were use to because they said they had all the bugs worked out of them.

Maggie started interviewing employees that could sew after fourteen applied from an add in the newspaper. She would hire five new employees, leaving one of the old machines free for whatever need might arise. A sales clerk also had to be hired for the front shop. A friend of Maggie's asked about a sales position, and Maggie hired her as manager of the front area. She had several years experience, and Maggie felt she was capable of taking charge after they had decided on some displays in the front windows and on the walls.

A large shipment of clothing should be arriving soon that was ordered from a spring clothing market that Maggie had attended in San Francisco. The clothing had been ordered for the fall and winter season because she knew she would be opening a shop soon, if not in Wilcottville, in the next town six miles away. She was very glad the one she found was suitable, as she liked being closer to home.

She was planning a grand opening. Zelma agreed to make the appetizers and be on hand to help for the two days. Julie said she would be glad to help out also, and had booked a lady in Sacramento that put on demonstrations on wearing scarfs for the opening. Some of the clothing would also be modeled by some of the employees and some of the town ladies that wanted to participate. Maggie was looking forward to a successful grand opening and business.

She had talked to Alice about being supervisor over the seamstresses, but Alice turned the position down because she didn't want to work longer hours or have the responsibility at her age. They both agreed that Jennifer could handle the job. So Maggie couldn't delay talking to Jennifer any longer and had invited her to lunch on Saturday at one of the better restaurants.

Maggie was too early as usual, and sat there thinking she could save herself some time if she didn't feel that she had to be early to all appointments. It was a habit she had automatically fallen into—something inside her subconscious that she couldn't seem to break. Her logical self told her she should be thankful to be this way instead of late all the time like some people she knew. Jennifer was right on time looking like a young executive in a beige summer suit. She greeted Maggie with a kiss on the cheek and seemed to be ecstatic about having lunch at such a 'swanky restaurant', as she called it.

"Well, I'm sorry to take you away from your family on a Saturday, Jennifer, but I have something important to talk to you about. Something I think you'll be excited about."

"Oh, tell me, what is it?" Jennifer eagerly asked in her usual clownish way. Her large dark brown eyes gleamed affectionately, making Maggie glad that she was also her friend. Maggie had vowed before she ever had any employees, not to become too involved in their personal lives, to keep only a business friendship, but with Alice and Jennifer, Maggie had fallen short of her promise and had grown very close to both of them.

"Jennifer, I want to offer you the position of being supervisor over the new seamstresses. I want you to know that I first offered this job to Alice, because she was my first employee, but she turned it down because she didn't want longer hours or the responsibility. She said she was too old."

"Oh, Maggie, do you think I know enough to handle it?"

"Yes, I do, Jennifer, but it depends on how you feel. I know you have a way with people. You're intelligent and have a lot of common sense. I really believe you can handle it and so does Alice. I'll be around most of the time to help, and Alice said she would be a back-up for you on any problem."

"Okay, it's settled, I'll do it," she squealed and started in on the Chef's salad that she had ordered for lunch.

"Fine. Now we have to work out a salary increase for you and some of the details of your responsibilities," Maggie told her and took a bite of her Cob salad. "I haven't had much time to think about this, Jennifer, but what I wish that we could both do over the weekend is make a list of-----".

"Maggie, Darling, how nice to see you again," Adrian Morgan's loud voice said, as she moved her wheel chair toward Maggie and Jennifer and extended her arms out.

Maggie hugged her and glanced up to see Jess talking to the hostess, than turned and walked toward them. "Adrian, you know Jennifer."

Adrian said something to Jennifer, but it was meaningless to Maggie, between the guilt she felt being near Adrian and the love she felt for Jess. It was like being torn apart, first one way and then the other.

"Hello, Jess," she said as he came near. I would also like you to meet Jennifer Schriber." She had talked so much about Jennifer and Alice to Jess that she knew Jess would know who she was.

"Hello, Jennifer, It's nice to meet you," Jess said, not mentioning that he knew her so well, even though he had never met her before.

"Jennifer has just consented to be supervisor over the new seamstresses for the shop," Maggie concluded.

"I read in the Wilcott Daily that you're opening a new shop. We certainly need a good one in this berg of a town," Adrian said, with a hint of sarcasm in her voice.

"Well, we hope to bring the women of this town what they want in the way of clothing," Maggie answered.

"Yes, our town is growing, as the old cliche goes, 'by leaps and bounds,' " Adrian went on, "And it's about time the women get out of their jeans and tee shirts and start dressing like women did twenty years ago."

Maggie glanced at Jess as he winked at her and smiled over his wife's comment.

"Adrian, I hope the other women of Wilcottville will share your views and patronize the shop regularly," Jennifer told her.

After Jess and Adrian went to their own table at the other end of the restaurant Maggie could hardly eat the salad she had ordered. Why did it upset her so much to see Jess and Adrian out together for lunch.

"Maggie, are you alright?" Jennifer asked, after Maggie had picked at her salad quietly, and had not returned to their unfinished conversation about the list.

"Oh, oh yes, I'm sorry, Jennifer. I just have a lot on my mind," she said, feeling slightly nauseated. Jess was so close and she couldn't touch him.

"The list----the list," Jennifer lightly teased.

"Yes, the list," answered Maggie laughing, trying to forget the ill at ease scene with Jess and Adrian. "Yes, I want you to make a list of what you think your duties should be as supervisor and what salary you expect. I'll do the same and we will get together Monday and compare them and put it into one.

The rest of their conversation during lunch was that of casual friends talking about their children and their hobbies. Their love for oil painting and horse back riding, which neither hardly ever had time to do, and they vowed that someday they would go horse back riding together and maybe even paint together someday. Maggie was glad to leave the restaurant before running into Adrian and Jess again. It was painful seeing them together and she knew she should end it with Jess. She didn't see how it would ever work out for them.

CHAPTER 7

Maggie was exhausted as she placed the last bolt of material on the storage shelf. A shipment had came in late this afternoon and she wanted to get it put away before she started working on the pile of book work setting on her desk. The employees had left for the day and Maggie thought it would be a quiet time to catch up on the book work and the bills.

Roby International kept asking her for a larger quantity of her designs, but she informed them she couldn't give them more than was designated in the contract right now. They wanted her to stop selling to other stores, which she planned on doing as soon as her contracts ran out. They also wanted all of her leather designs to go under their trademark, offering her a substantial amount of money. The amount was so staggering that she had decided to do that. She would still have "Designs By Meg" in the material clothing.

Maggie glanced at her watch as she heard a knock at the back door. It was almost five thirty, and she couldn't imagine a delivery coming this late. "Yes, who is it?" she called to the person on the other side of the solid heavy door.

"U.P.S. , Ma'am Three boxes here for a Maggie Lancing from Volks, Inc.."

She was expecting this shipment of merchandise and quickly unbolted the door. "Thank you. Just put the boxes over there please."

"Sign here on line twelve," the young man said and handed her the clip board. "Thank you and have a nice evening," he said as he disappeared out the door.

She looked at the boxes. Dare she open them and peek at the new clothing. She was so tired and she needed to get to the book work, but she couldn't resist opening one box before returning to the books.

Maggie looked at the clock which now read eight thirty eight and decided to quit for the night. She unplugged the coffee pot and was cleaning her desk off when she heard the back door open. Fear stabbed her as she remembered not bolting the door after the U.P.S. delivery man left. She peeked through the office door and saw Julio looking around the room.

Feeling the need to panic she reassured herself she could handle this. If she kept quiet maybe he wouldn't look in the small office. If he took some clothing, she didn't care, just so he didn't find her. She reached for the sharp letter opener, the only weapon she had, wishing she had listened to Jess and took the small hand gun he had offered her. Why had she so carelessly left the heavy back door unlocked. She heard Julio walk to the front of the store. The night lights were on and someone could see him through the windows if they went by the store. He didn't stay long in the front and she heard him coming to the back again. Seeing no one around he started taking the new clothes out of the opened box. Dare she try to reach the phone on the desk for help. She would only have time to dial the operator and what if the operator didn't answer immediately and Julio heard her.

He started walking toward the office. She raised her hand holding the letter opener as Julio appeared in the doorway. She hid behind the door, but he pulled it forward, "Ah! Miss Maggie, here you are," He laugh. The stench of alcohol and cigarettes consumed him. "I've been waiting for you to stay late every night by yourself."

"Huleo stay away from me. Please don't cause anymore trouble or I swear I'll call the police this time."

"Oh, come now, Miss Maggie, you won't do that, because you then will know what will happened to your beautiful daughter," he said in his broken Spanish accent.

"Huleo, what do you hope to accomplish from all this? You're only causing trouble for yourself and your family," Maggie told him in a scared nervous voice.

He grabbed for her arm which held the letter opener, but Maggie was faster and jabbed his lower arm with it. "You bitch!" he hollered, and held his arm while the blood started to slowly drip from it.

Maggie saw the chance to run for the back door, but the clothes he had scattered around kept catching on her heels. Her assailant tackled her around the waist pulling her down on the floor, while the blood from his arm was getting all over Maggie and the new shipment of clothes underneath them. She screamed as loud as she could while Julio put his hand over her mouth. She bit his hand and he swore and threatened her again. He twisted her wrist making her drop the letter opener.

"I'll teach you to bite me, bitch," he said, as he ripped the buttons off down the front of her blouse breaking her bra strap also, and exposing one of her breast. A strange look crossed his face and his dark eyes shined with a lustful desire as he glared at Maggie's breast.

"Please let me go, Huleo. Please don't touch me. I'll give you money and clothes-----what ever you want," she cried.

"Shut up, bitch, or I'll use this knife on you and cut you up in pieces."

Suddenly the back door opened and Jess stood there with an astonished look on his face at what he saw.

"Jess, Jess, oh thank Heavens!"

"What the hell are you doing?" Jess asked as he hurried toward them.

Huleo quickly stood up and reached for his knife in its holster, but Jess hit him with a right, knocking him back against some boxes. Jess picked him up by his shirt collar.

"You dirty filthy Mexican," He said, as he hit him with another right in the face. Not only was his arm still bleeding slowly from the paper opener, but now his nose and a cut above his eye was also bleeding. Huleo backed away when Jess started toward him again.

"Wait, I will go. I don't want any trouble," he pleaded.

"Well, it looks like you're the one causing it. Call the police, Maggie."

"Jess, I can't," she hesitated. "The publicity. What would it look like? And he's threatened to hurt Julie if I turn him in."

"Maggie, this creep was about to rape you when I walked in, maybe even kill you."

"No, no, I wouldn't hurt her," Julio pleaded again. I only want to get even with Bill for firing me."

"You deserved to get fired, Julio, you're an alcoholic. Get help before it's too late," Maggie yelled at him.

"I promise I will get help. Just let me go," he answered while he dabbed the blood on his face and arm with a new blouse he had picked up off the floor.

"What about this mess you caused? These are new clothes that you ruined with blood stains," Jess told him.

Julio was silent as he looked around at the scattered blood stained clothing on the floor.

"Well, It's up to you, Maggie, what do you want to do with him?"

"Let him out the back door. Julio, don't ever try this again. And if you in anyway hurt my daughter you'll pay for it with your life," Maggie told him loudly.

"I hope you understand that, because your life won't be worth a plug nickle if you don't," Jess told him as he pushed him out the door and locked and bolted it.

Jess looked at Maggie, "How did he get in here?"

"I forgot to lock the door after the UPS man brought a shipment in."

"I hope this isn't a mistake letting him go. He could get nasty," he said.

"I don't think he will try it again, Jess, now that he knows that you know too. And I couldn't get you involved in this. It would be in the papers and all over town. I only hope he hasn't tried to rape any other women. But I think we would have heard around this small town if he had.

"Has he tried this before, Maggie, with you?"

She hesitated for a few seconds, "Yes, the time the colt got cut up and you had to suture him,"

"Is that what was wrong with you that day? I always wondered. What did he do to you?"

 Maggie didn't answer. She hung her head. "Did he rape you?"

"Yes," she cried, as she remembered that day so vividly. "He pounded my head against the barn floor and I blacked out. He was gone when I came to and the colt was caught in the fence.

"Oh Maggie, why didn't you tell me then," he said, as he pulled her into his arms.

"I was afraid you would either try to kill him or go to the police. He can be dangerous and I didn't want you to get hurt. And he threatened to hurt Julie if I called the police or told anyone.

"You poor thing." Still holding her, he said, "You went through that terrible ordeal all alone."

"No, you were there and you held me, even though you didn't know why I was upset. I wanted to tell you so badly, but I couldn't get you involved."

"I'll always be here for you. Please don't ever keep anything from me again," he told her while they still clung to each other.

"It's getting late. Come on let's clean this mess up." Jess said as he started picking up the clothes. "What should we do with the blood stain clothes?"

"Hum—that's a good question. I don't want the employees to know anything about this."

"I could take the clothes and burn them in my incinerator at the clinic."

"Good idea on these bad stained pieces. But the rest of the clothing I can send to the cleaners and give them to the mission," Maggie told him.

Forty minutes later the back room looked the same as before. Even the blood stains on the carpet came up with a special cleaner, leaving no evidence of blood anywhere. Maggie had changed her clothes and sat down on a chair exhausted from her hectic day. Jess started to pull up another chair from a sewing machine near by, but changed his mind sticking his hands in his pockets he paced the floor.

"Maggie, you must be very careful about being alone and locking doors. And check your car before you get into it. In fact keep it locked."

"I will, Jess, I promise."

"I really don't think Julio will bother you again, unless he gets so drunk he doesn't know what he's doing, then who can tell what he may do. I'll bring you a hand gun tomorrow for protection, but be very careful with it."

"Jess, I really don't think I need one. I think I can handle this now. I worry about Julie, but I really think he's too scared to do anything to her, especially since he knows now that you know about him."

"Well, I hope your right." Maggie pulled her hair back and twisted it into a bun, "Jess, I'm just so glad that you did come by tonight." She took the pins that had fallen out of her hair and repined it.

"You know it's odd. I just felt this urgent need to see you and I thought you might be here." he said, as he extended his arm out to Maggie pulling her up out of the chair. "We better go home and get some rest."

"Good idea. I'm so tired," Maggie said, as she put her arms around Jess's neck. "Thanks for coming, for saving my life." She kissed him and he pulled her tighter too him.

"If anything happened to you, Darling, I don't know what I would do. Please be careful."

"Jess, that day I seen you and Adrian at the restaurant I had second thoughts about going on with this, but how can I let you go. I would die if I couldn't talk to you and see you.

He kissed her again. Not passionate, but in a loving way. "Can we get away to Sacramento in a few weeks?" Maggie asked while she was still in his arms.

"I would like nothing better than that. Let me check my schedule. I just purchased some land to build the new clinic on and I have a lot meetings and paper work to sign to get the new building started."

"Oh, Jess, that's wonderful. Where's the land located?"

"Out on the old River Creek Road. I bought ten acres out there and have some fence builders already fencing it in and building a small stable to keep the sick horses in."

"That's a pretty drive out that way. I'm very happy that you found it."

Maggie grabbed her purse and they went out the door locking it securely. Jess had made sure no one was around to see them leave the shop together and go to their own cars.

Maggie was very busy for the next month after getting the shop organized and helping Jennifer work out some problems with the seamstresses. She also helped her new manager in the front sales area get started and they hired another sales clerk to work there. Maggie hoped to work out all the beginning problems of starting a new business, so that her two managers could take over and she could spend most of her time designing her line of clothing, and of course doing the book work until she could afford to hire a bookkeeper.

Her and Jess both had been too busy to get away together to Sacramento. Jess was busy with all the details of building a new animal clinic, but they did keep in touch once in awhile on the phone. A month and half after the incident at the shop with Julio, Jess called her on his way back to the animal clinic.

"Maggie, are you sitting down?"

"Jess, what's wrong? Yes, I'm sitting down. What is it?" She sounded frightened.

Julio was just killed in a car accident. I came upon the accident and several people had already stopped, but didn't know what to do. I helped him the best I could, but he was hurt to bad. He was crushed to bad to live. He did say something to me, Maggie. He must have recognized me, because he said. 'tell Maggie to forgive'.

Maggie gasp. "Are you alright?" Jess asked her.

"Was there another car involved?"

"No, he hit a tree head on. He must have been drunk. The smell of liquor on him was strong and the officer found a bottle in his car."

"Oh Jess, what about his family?" Maggie asked.

"I know, but maybe they're better off without him. Well, I don't know, it's hard to say. We don't really know their situation," Jess answered her.

"I'll go see his wife to see what I can do for them," Maggie said. "I can't go to the funeral though, not after what he did. I'll wait until after the funeral to see her. She may need a job."

"Maggie, I'll call you later. Will you be okay? Don't let this get you upset. I love you."

"I'm okay. I love you too. Bye Jess."

Maggie went to see Julio's wife, Angelina, three days after the funeral. She didn't know what to expect. But didn't expect to find them in such poverty as what she did. Their furnishings in the small home were shabby and nothing was very clean. They had some food leftover from the funeral that the other Mexican families had brought to them. But their old refrigerator was almost bare and the cupboards too. They didn't have a phone and Maggie assured Angelina that she would call the grocery market when she got home and have them deliver enough food for two weeks.

Angelina cried and hugged Maggie.

"Bless you, bless you, God must have sent you," she told her. She could not speak English very well, but the older children helped Maggie understand their mother's words. She told Maggie that they were not much better off before her husband's death. He only got a small unemployment check and spent a lot of it on liquor. He abused all of them and they were glad when he wasn't home.

"Do you know how to sew on a machine ?" Maggie asked Angelina.

"Sew? Machine?" Angelina asked, not knowing what it was.

"No, she doesn't, only by hand she can sew," the oldest daughter, who looked to be about seventeen, answered.

"Would you like a job sewing for me on a machine? I can teach you." Maggie asked, and looked at the daughter to interpret for her.

The daughter spoke in Spanish to her mother, and listened to her before she returned the message to Maggie.

"She would if she could be trained," the daughter said.

"Tell her I can start teaching her next week at my shop down town, if you kids will teach her English at night. Will you do that?" asked Maggie.

"Yes, we will do that," several of the older children answered.

"Did your husband have insurance on his car?" Maggie asked.

"No, no insurance. No more car," Angelina told her sadly.

"You need a car to get around in. We have an old car that was my sons, just sitting at home. He's away at college. You can have it. And I'll see that one of the farm workers brings it over with the title to put it in your name. Now," She turned to the oldest girls, " Do you have your license?"

"Yes, we both do."

"Good. Are you both still in high school?" Maggie kept asking questions

"Yes, me and Marie are both seniors. I'm Marta. Richard is a sophomore and the other three are still in grammar school," Marta answered.

"Would you and Marie like to go to college?"

"We have no money to go," Marie answered her.

"Well, let me get started on some arrangements and try to get some scholarships going for you both," Maggie told them, while they smiled with delight. "Now than, you could drive your mother to work before school, couldn't you?" she asked.

"Yes, yes," they answered.

Angelina and the two older girls hugged Maggie as she was leaving, and told her thank you over and over again. Their gratitude was obvious, and Maggie felt good doing something to help others. She also made a mental note to go to the mission and see about getting them all some clothes, and to remember to call the market as soon as she got home to deliver them groceries.

CHAPTER 8

Maggie and Jess had not been able to get together for several months. They had talked on the phone about once a week to keep in touch and keep up on necessary events. Now they were both able to get away from their busy schedules, and had met in "Old Sacramento" walking through the streets and then to a restaurant where they were sure that no one they knew would be at through the week days.

It was a cloudy rainy day and they watched the clouds move from the large window by their table. They sipped on Cappuccino, relaxing after enjoying a light lunch, and drinking in the closeness of each other which they so seldom had. Maggie's eyes were shining as she watched Jess's every move, savoring this in her memory for the hundreds of hours they could not be together, and glowing in the fact that she was hopelessly in love with him.

"Look at me," Jess demanded her, as Maggie met his soft gaze. "God! You're beautiful today," he told her, as he took her hands in his.

"It's because I'm in love with the most wonderful man in the world."

"Well, you do have a special shine in your deep blue eyes and a glow on your face since we've been together that could contribute to being in love."

"I am, but enough of that. I'll prove it to you later tonight. I keep forgetting to ask you how the new clinic is coming along when we talk on the phone. It seems like we're always in a hurry when we talk."

Jess took a sip from his cup. "It's coming along very well. It should be finished, at least I'm hoping, by the end of November. It's huge compared to my little clinic I now have. Plenty of yard space for parking and pens for boarding animals outside as well as inside.

"What's the interior like?" Maggie asked, while affectionately rubbing Jess' arm.

"Oh, a lot of rooms. Mostly all white. A large waiting room with four small rooms for the animal patients to be examined in. The floors are all tile. I have a good sized office and my office manager has an office, and than an office in the waiting room area. You'll have to come see it. We'll have an open house later on.

"I will," Maggie answered, "When you say it's okay."

"I wish you could decorate the walls for me, but that might be a little suspicious to my staff," he told her. "Your shop is so beautiful."

"Thank you. The grand opening went over very well. We had a big crowd for the two days. Zelma, my cook, made the appetizers, and I had Angelina's daughters, Marie and Marta, serve them. They are such nice girls, Jess. I really enjoy being with them. I'm working with their high school counselor on getting scholarships for them to go to college. And Angelina is becoming an excellent seamstress. She wants to please so much and is so greatful for the job. I tell her it's okay, that I needed someone like her to sew for me, but she is so gracious."

"Maggie, you are unbelievable. Here this guy rapes you and almost kills you twice and you turn around and give his wife a job and get his kids into college. I'm not belittling you for it, it's amazing. I love you for it," he laugh," "You've got guts."

"Well, they had nothing. No money, no food, hardly any clothes, no car, nothing. It really makes a better person of me, and maybe the Lord won't be so hard on me because I love you."

"I'm sorry to make you feel guilty about us. I do too if it's any consolation," Jess told her while taking her hand again in his.

Maggie leaned toward Jess, "Are we wasting out time here? I want to be closer to you," she whispered.

They walked into the luxurious motel room and Maggie sat her small garment bag down. She took out some clothing, and hung a dress in the closet that she would wear tomorrow.

"Jess, I would like to shower. I feel like I have all the sidewalk dust of 'Old Sacramento' on me."

"Do you mind if I join you?" He asked, while pulling the bed covers back.

"Do you think I mind?" Maggie asked, undressing and wrapping a large towel around her body. She was already soapy all over and started rubbing soap on Jess when he entered the shower. He gathered her in his arms.

"It's been so long, Maggie."

She felt his hardness press against her, and a desire rush through her while she waited for his lips to consume hers as she melted against him.

Afterwards they both slid to the shower floor exhausted, with cool shower water beating against them. Finally Jess spoke, still out of breath, "Darling, I can't believe it's this good with you."

"I never dreamed it could be this way," Maggie agreed, "but I believe it's because our love is so great."

"I believe you're right," Jess teased, and kiss the end of her nose in a gesture of love.

They finally got enough energy to finish their shower and Maggie slipped into a long white lace nightgown, than into bed. Jess got under the covers beside her and she moved closer cuddling up in his arms.

"It's so nice to hold you," he murmured, smoothing her hair back and outlining her face with his index finger. "Are you sleepy?"

"No, I just want to savor this precious time with you, and try not to feel guilty at the same time," she answered. "Does Adrian trust you?"

"I think so. She jokingly brings up something about women from time to time. Maybe she really doesn't want to know. I only wish it were different for her, Maggie. I mean----to never enjoy sex again—that's hard. I know a women's sexual desires are not quite as strong as a man's, but a man lives for it, probably above anything else."

"Jess, you went for a long time without sex."

"Over eight long years. I put all my energy into my work, but then you came along and I fell hook, line and sinker. It was never very good with Adrian and me. Not like it is with us. I don't think she ever really enjoyed it very much. She wouldn't open up and tell me what her desires were."

"Bill either. It was like he thought I really didn't want to enjoy it. Like only men should and women should have no desires."

"Did Adrian come to your grand opening?" Jess asked.

"Yes, her nurse brought her. She bought quite a few items of clothing. And yes, I feel guilty as can be when I see her. I just want to go hide and cry. What will we do, Jess? We can't keep going on like this?"

"Do you have a solution? I don't," he said , and pounded the pillow in frustration. "If I have to give you up I'll die. And at the same time I don't want to hurt Adrian. It would kill her to find out. I know I'm deceiving her, but what can we do?"

"Oh, Jess, I know how it is. I can't hurt Bill either. But I can't live without you. Maybe we shouldn't talk on the phone so much and just meet every six months. If I know you will always love me no matter what, I can do it."

"Okay, if you can do it, I guess I can get by also without seeing you as much. There's only one thing, Christmas will be here in several months and I told you last Christmas that we would be together next Christmas, remember? I don't mean on Christmas day, but a few days before."

"Okay, Jess, we can get together just before Christmas . That's such a special time, and I really want to spend some of it with you. After that, how can we wait until June to be together again?"

"Instead of taking a week at a time we'll take a month at a time. And yes, I will always love you. No matter what happens," Jess told her before kissing her passionately.

"This is so much fun laying in your arms like this, forgetting everything else. How can we give this up?" she asked. She massaged his chest and curled her fingers around the dark hair covering it.

It was so peaceful in their room. The only sound was a babbling brook from a water fall inside the room. The noise was soothing and added to the beautiful room. Their bed was king size and a living room group graced the other end of the large room. Jess massaged Maggie's neck. "I saw some hand creme in the bathroom. I'll get it and give you a massage," he told her while jumping out of bed and returning with the creme. "Have to take your gown off first and turn over on your stomach," he ordered her gently. After massaging her back side, Maggie was so relaxed she turned over while Jess continued the massage on her front side, finding places that made her catch her breath. She felt her heart beat faster and looked at Jess knowing he was studying her changing expressions closely. Their gaze locked and she felt his rapid heartbeat as well as her own. He drew her necked body against his own and sought her trembling lips as they were lost in time that only lovers exist in.

They stayed in bed until evening, playfully acting like teenagers and dreading the time they would have to part. "I think I've worked up an appetite. How about you? Let's go find a nice restaurant," Jess told her.

"Sounds great, I'm starved too," Maggie answered.

They chose a restaurant that looked like a huge cabin in the woods. The landscape was interesting, with a lot of old pine trees and rocks around making it look like it was actually hidden in the forest. After they were seated Jess decided he would find a coat rack to hang his jacket on. He didn't return for sometime and Maggie was getting concerned. She had already looked over the menu twice and decided what she would have.

"Maggie, what in the world are you doing here by yourself?" She heard someone say. Looking up she recognized Lois Montgomery, an acquaintance from Wilcottville.

"Hello, Lois," she managed, hoping Jess would see the situation and not return to the table yet. I'm just here on a business trip," she smiled.

Lois continued talking for awhile and than excused herself to return to her table. Jess still was not back. She glanced around the restaurant and saw Jess beckoning to her from an area closer to the front entry. She knew immediately he must have ran into Lois or her husband and wanted to leave.

He grabbed her arm, "Let's get out of here. I ran into Ted Montgomery in the lobby. They're sitting right over there," he said, pointing to a table just beyond the one where Maggie and Jess had been.

"Lois came by our table and spoke to me also," Maggie told him on the way to the car. "She asked me what I was doing there all alone, and I told her I was here on a business trip."

They got close to their car and noticed it was parked in view of the window where the Montgomerys were sitting. "Maggie, walk back to the entrance and I'll circle around the restaurant and pick you up there," he told her.

"Whee----that was close. Good thing I went looking for that coat rack or they would have caught us together," Jess said, as Maggie got into the car.

"Do you think they will suspect anything after seeing both of us at the same restaurant?" she asked.

"I hope not," Jess said, as he sped away to look for another restaurant. "Ted said they were there celebrating their anniversary. That's why they were there on a weekday."

They drove several miles around Sacramento before they saw a restaurant that looked inviting. "This is a good steak house and I know they have excellent prime rib here. Nobody should be here that we know today," Jess told her and pulled into the parking lot.

Inside the beamed ceiling was very high throughout the whole restaurant. A wide rustic stairway led to a top level that overlooked the tables below. The delicious smell of steaks cooking over a large open barbeque pit in the middle of the restaurant made their mouths water and they realized how hungry they were.

They had coffee after dinner holding hands on the table. Jess looked into Maggie's eyes, "I hate for this day to end. It was wonderful, except for running into our friends at the other restaurant," he said, while they both laugh quietly at the incident.

"Where about do Julie and Steve live here in Sacramento?"

"On the north side. It's close to his dad's manufacturing business."

"Is everything going well with them? You haven't mention them lately," Jess asked, rubbing her arm as though he couldn't get enough of the feel of her soft creamy skin.

Maggie laid her hand on his arm that was touching hers. Why couldn't they be together all time she thought. No, they had obligations and would have to take things one at a time. A month at a time as Jess' had suggested. Maggie collected her thought and returned to Jess question.

Julie is anxious to start a family, but realizes she must finish college first and get established in her career before having a baby. I don't think Steve is quiet as anxious for a family yet."

"And how's college going for Jonathan?"

"I think it's going well. He calls home once a week on Saturday or Sunday. I think maybe he gets a little homesick from time to time," Maggie answered. "I sure miss him. He works six hours after school and some weekends in a fast food restaurant."

"Well, that's good experience for him. Working with the public and his colleagues in a restaurant is some of the best experience he could get to be an attorney."

"Yes, I suppose so. Some of those kids that work in that type of restaurant probably cause a lot of problems for everyone and have a lot of problems of their own also." Maggie said. "He said a lot of times the kids don't show up for work and they call him to come in. So he does get a lot of hours in and it gives him spending money. He just bought another car and has payments to make on it."

The waitress poured hot coffee into their empty cups . Jess took a sip before resuming the conversation. "I suppose you do really worry about him. Being on his own and all,"

"I do, but he is a good boy. I pray for him and turn it over to God to protect him. I feel at peace about him then and confident that God will take care of him," Maggie answered.

"Again I'm telling you that you are amazing. You're beautiful on the inside, Maggie. I love you so much," he leaned across the table and kissed her gently. "I pray for Cris and his family too. I think every things going okay for them. He has a good job as manager with a computer firm. His wife is a little bossy, but they seem to get along well."

"I imagine the babies are growing. How old are they now?"

"The boy is three years and the little girl two," he answered.

"Goodness the time goes by fast. It seems like you told me the little girl was just born."

"Yeah, I've been a grandpa for three years now. They call me PaPa. I don't get to see them much since they moved to the Bay area. The time sure flies by when we're busy. Won't be long and some little ones will be running around calling you grandma," Jess laugh.

"I hope not for awhile. For three or four years anyway," she smiled. "It will be nice to have grandchildren though when the time is ready. I just want Julie to have a good start first. She wants to come into the clothing business with me someday, but I think she needs to get some experience in another career first."

"Good idea. You're not only beautiful inside and out, but smart too," He laugh and nudged her playfully.

"Oh quit teasing me, grandpa," she told him and punched him lightly on the shoulder.

" What am I going to do without you until Christmas?" He ask, as he looked into her eyes.

"That isn't too far away. But than what will we do until next June? Six months without you," she tearfully said.

"Let's go up to Lake Tahoe in June. The weather will be beautiful. And we can go boating and fishing and gamble a little in the casinos. See a floor show. I'll try to get Adrian to visit her family in Arizona, than I could come up for four or five days if you could get away that long," he said excitedly.

"That sounds wonderful, and I probably could get away that long. It will be something to look forward to after Christmas."

They drove back to the motel so Maggie could get her car. Jess kissed her longingly, and they clung to each other for a long time before Maggie pulled away and got into her car and drove off.

CHAPTER 9

1984

Fall was coming to an end with the approach of the thanksgiving holiday. The yellow and red leaves were falling leaving the trees almost stripped bare. The evenings turned dark by five thirty, and the stock had to be fed earlier.

Maggie had left the shop early today and was sitting in front of the fireplace in her living room, feeling cozy watching the dagger like flames whip through the logs. She was reminiscing about the past Christmas' and felt the anticipation of the holidays drawing near. It would be wonderful to spend Christmas day with Jess, but her own family needed her. It just wouldn't be Christmas without Bill and the children and their families, and also her parents and Bills. What would they think if they knew she, trustworthy Maggie, had a lover. She felt as though she was living two lives. Tears came to her eyes. Perhaps she had made her own life more miserable by letting things happen that could have been avoided.

Guilt swept over her as she realized it had been five years now since their affair started. They only met every six months like they had agreed to, but the wait in between was almost unbearable for both of them. There was little chance that their dream of a married life together would come true, Maggie felt. It was as though fate was against them with a crippled wife and a ranch that Maggie could never take away from Bill, even though most of it she had inherited from her family. How much longer could they both go on living with unfaithfulness and deceit.

Maggie closed her eyes blocking out the guilt and imagined Jess's arms around her. She could smell the cologne he often wore and the clean odor of an antiseptic he used a lot on the animals he doctored. Silver Bells was playing on the stereo, and she wondered how she and Jess would celebrate their own private Christmas and exchange their gifts this year.

The shrill ring of the phone shook Maggie back to the present. "Darling, I called the shop and they said you had left early, so thought I could catch you at home."

"Jess, it seems like it's been forever since I heard from you," Maggie said, as she turned the stereo volume down.

"Two months to be exact," Jess answered. "I've been very busy, Maggie. Operations, meetings, a mad horse owner, you name it and I've been through it lately."

"Oh, I'm sorry to hear that, Jess, sounds like you have been through it."

"I just wanted to call you before Thanksgiving and say 'Hi' , and was hoping we could get together a week before Christmas to shop and have a nice cozy dinner somewhere."

"I was just sitting here wondering what we would do this Christmas. Do you realize, Jess, that we've been together five years?"

"Yes, but it seems like I've always loved you," he answered.

"Me too," Maggie quietly said.

"I thought we might go to Sacramento to one of the malls and then have a nice dinner, and spend the night there," he added.

"Sounds great, Darling. I'm really looking forward to it."

"We're going to my son's home for Thanksgiving. I'll be thinking of you."

"Everyone is coming here for the holiday this year. The kids and their spouses and my parents and Bills. But I'll be thinking of you too."

"I have to go, Maggie. My assistant has another animal patient for me to doctor. I love you. Can't wait to see you."

"Bye Jess, I love you too and can't wait to be with you."

Thanksgiving was hectic as usual with a houseful of people. Jonathan was an attorney in southern California now, and he and his new bride of one year were expecting a baby in May. Julie and Steve still had not started a family. Julie was getting impatient, but Steve kept putting it off. Maggie's parents were not in very good health. They were middle aged when Maggie and her brother were born and they were in their late seventy's now. Bill's parents were healthy except his father had arthritis and walked with a cane. Zelma was still with them and had cooked most of the Thanksgiving dinner, except for Maggie's special recipes she made every year.

"Oh this turkey is delicious," exclaimed Jonathan. "It's great to come home for Thanksgiving and see all of you, and have this great dinner and than the leftovers," he said, laughing. "Mom, you promised to give Lorie some of your recipes, and Zelma said she would show her how to make those great banana pancakes in the morning for breakfast."

Maggie's dad laugh, "sounds like you haven't been eating too good, my boy."

"I never learned how to cook too well," Lorie said embarrassed.

"Well, by the time you leave here Sunday you'll know quite a bit about cooking, because Zelma and I are going to teach both you and Jonathan a lot over the next three days," Maggie told her.

"Maggie, how is your shop doing?" her mother-in-law asked.

"Very well," she answered. "We are so busy. You know I lease the building next door when it came up vacant and tore the wall down to expand. Our sewing department is in that building now and we have ten people sewing for us. Julie is starting to work for us next month. She's going to manage some of the larger company sales and use her expertise in art to do some designing."

"Well, my goodness, you just have all kinds of things going on there. Designing and sewing, and sells to companies plus selling to the public there. No wonder we never see you, Maggie," the older women told her while taking a helping of cranberries.

"I really am sorry I don't get to see all of you more. It does keep me busy. To busy, but I wanted a business."

"Thank Heavens for holidays," Maggie's mother added, "or we would never get to see any of you."

"Isn't that the truth," Bill added, "I hardly ever see Maggie anymore than any of you do."

His father frowned at him. "Oh, Bill, you're so busy with your cattle and orchards and hay fields, you're never home before dark anyway."

"You got that right. It keeps me busy," he answered. "And Maggie and I are both so tired at night, we eat and hit the hay."

Maggie glanced at Steve. "I'll try not to work Julie too many hours, Steve. "It may be more through the Christmas holidays, and then she can work the hours she wants to."

"So you're going to give up the speech therapist job, Julie?" asked her paternal grandmother.

"Yes, Mother has offered me more money and I think the clothing business will be something interesting to get into. I can always go back into speech therapy later if I want."

"How is your business going, Steve?" One of the grandfathers asked.

"Okay. Towards the end of the year it always starts to slow down. During the winter months. But it will pick up in the spring," he answered.

"And Jonathan, how do you like this lawyer business?" asked his other grandfather.

Jonathan laugh at the way he asked. "Well, it's a profession. I have a lot to learn yet. I work for a great firm. There's five attorneys there and I'm the new Junior one. They all give me pointers from time to time. Experiences they already had."

"Well, just try to stay honest, grandson." Maggie's dad told him. "And the Lord will look after you."

"And Lorie, what do you do?" Bill's mother asked.

"I work in the office where Jonathan works. That's how we met," she answered before taking a bite of mashed potatoes. She swallowed. "We didn't tell them that we were dating, but than we had to tell them when we decided to get married. They didn't know if they wanted a husband and wife working in the same office, but they didn't want to lose either one of us so they said it would be alright for us both to stay."

"Everyone save room for pumpkin and pecan pie," Maggie told them.

"Oh, we're so full," complained Jonathan.

"We can have that later in the living room with coffee," Maggie answered.

Maggie wrote Bill a note telling him she had a dinner meeting in Sacramento and would be home late or maybe even stay overnight with a lady friend, and for him to not worry about her. It was Zelma's day off so Maggie left him dinner of meat loaf, baked potato and green beans in the warm oven and tossed salad in the refrigerator. Bill never seemed to suspect anything and Maggie wondered how he could be so naive. She didn't go out of town very much now like she use to when she was first starting her business and had so much PR work to do. She supposed he had become accustomed to it from that time and was happy that he didn't get suspicious. It probably never crossed his mind that there could be someone else in her life. He either trusted her or maybe he really didn't care. Oh well, it was easier this way. She didn't have to tell more lies to cover up.

Maggie straightened her grey wool suit before opening the front office door to the animal clinic. Jess looked up from the filing cabinet in the main office. Laying the folder in his hand on top of the cabinet he walked to the counter.

"Glad to see you, Maggie," he said, as he winked at her. He turned to his office manager who was putting her coat on when Maggie walked in. "Janice, you take off early as we already discussed and get some of your Christmas shopping done, because I can help Maggie and I'm leaving in just a little while myself."

"Alright, but I can help Maggie before I go," she volunteered.

"Oh no, no, Janice," Maggie answered nervously, "I just wanted to discuss something about one of the horses with Dr. Morgan."

"Well, you both have a nice evening, and I'll see you Monday morning, Doctor."

Janice disappeared out the door, and Jess walked over to it locking the door before he pulled Maggie into his arms.

"Oh it's good to see you." He said and gently kissed her. "I love you so much. I hope you never get tired of hearing that, because I'm going to tell you that for the rest of our lives."

Maggie brushed his hair back off his forehead, "Never will I get tired of hearing that, Darling. You have my permission to repeat it forever and ever," she laugh.

With all the clinic employees gone for the day, they put Maggie's car behind the buildings where it couldn't be seen from the driveway. The sky was already beginning to turn dark and rain clouds were gathering in the North-West as they drove out of town toward Sacramento.

"Looks like a storm is brewing to the North," Jess said, as he looked toward the clouds through the windshield.

"A cozy night to go shopping and have dinner with a good looking doctor," Maggie smiled, putting her arm around the back of his neck as they sped out of town.

"Maggie, I can't tell you how happy you make me feel when we are together. It's rainbows and flowers and pure white snow."

"Spring time and Magnolias," Maggie laugh, joining in. "Oh, Jess, I've never been so happy before either. The depression returns when I'm not with you, but I work hard at the shop to forget it, and looking forward to seeing you again keeps me going. But you know this has to end sometime."

"No, I'll never let you go, no matter what happens. I couldn't live without you now."

"And your wife can't live without you, Jess. We have to be realistic. And we're not. We're just fooling ourselves in thinking that things will change and we'll be able to get married. We're both married----unhappily, but married."

"Do you want me to kill her, Maggie? What do you want?" He asked in despair.

"No, of course not. I'm just concerned about someone finding out. What it would do to Adrian and Bill if they knew. What it would do to us, our families," she answered somberly.

"Maggie, tonight there's only us. Let's enjoy each other's company. God only knows we work hard enough at our jobs trying to please others all the time. And trying to please Adrian is Hell in it's self. She threw a hot bowl of soup at the nurse the other day. It was a good thing I was home when it happened because it burned the nurses' arm and she went into shock. I felt like throwing Adrian over my lap and spanking her."

"What did you do?" asked Maggie.

"Well I doctored the nurse and sent her home early. I hope she doesn't file a lawsuit against us. It wasn't a very bad burn, but I know that hurt having a hot bowl of soup thrown on you all of a sudden. Adrian apologized to her and said she would never do anything like that again. I think it scared Adrian. I hope it did anyway. I hope it scared her enough she'll think twice before she throws a fit a again."

"I can see why you have a hard time keeping nurses. Does she ever throw things at you?"

"Oh Yeah! Several weeks ago I handed her a glass of tomato juice. Well she had asked for orange juice and I absent mindedly gave her tomato, and she threw the glass at me. Red tomato juice went all over the beige carpeting. The housekeeper was gone and I had a heck of a time getting that red color up from that light carpet."

Jess drove to a mall in the North area of Sacramento where they wouldn't be so apt to run into anyone from home. The large mall was full of busy Christmas shoppers hurrying to do their last minute shopping, with Christmas only a week away. The mall was beautifully decorated. The nostalgia of Christmas filled the air with a pure white Merry-go-round dotted with small white sparkling lights. Beautiful old fashioned dressed porcelain dolls rode on the horses. In another scene Santa and his Elves were feeding hay to Rudolph and the other reindeer. Colored lights on Christmas trees throughout the mall added to the beauty of the season.

"Jess, It's Christmas and we're together. Oh I love this season!" Maggie's blue eyes sparkled. "Isn't the mall just beautiful. They really went all out. I can just feel the magic of Christmas coming alive," she told him as she put her arm through his. "Part of the magic is being with you."

"I want you to help me pick out a gift in this jewelry store for the most beautiful and wonderful women in the whole world," Jess said, as he steered her into the most expensive jewelry store in the mall.

"What can I help you with today?" the clerk asked as Maggie and Jess looked over the diamond and pearl jewelry in the show case.

"Oh Jess, it's all so expensive," Maggie exclaimed, as they both absent mindedly ignored the clerk's question.

"Nothing is to expensive for you," Jess answered as he squeezed her shoulders. "Do you like this diamond and pearl necklace?" he asked, pointing to probably the most expensive piece of jewelry in that particular case.

"Oh, I love it. Are you sure, Jess?" She asked excitedly, as the clerk unlocked the back of the glass case and took the piece of jewelry out. "Oh, it's beautiful," Maggie said, as she held the necklace up to get a better look at it.

"I think she likes it," Jess winked at the clerk. "We'll take it. Do you want to wear it?" he looked at Maggie questionably.

"Oh yes, I do," she answered, handing it back to the clerk so that the price tag could be removed first. "No, wait. I can't take this, Jess, it isn't right."

"Maggie, nothing is more right than for me to want to give you a Christmas present." Jess put the necklace on her and said it looked stunning with her grey wool suit and silk ivory blouse, all designs she had created. He reached into the inside top pocket of his jacket and pulled cash out to pay for the necklace.

After they left the jewelry store Maggie squeezed his hand. "Thank you, Darling, this is the best present I've ever received from anyone." Than hesitating a minute she asked, "Jess, do you usually carry that much cash around with you?"

"No, silly, I planned on spending that on your present. I thought it best not to write a check in case it got into the wrong hands. I wish we didn't have to go to large towns and sneak around to out of the way places, but I don't know what we should do about it right now. I want everyone in the world to know I love you, but we will have to settle for just knowing we love each other for now. And what the future brings we'll face when the time comes."

"How much longer can we both go on with the lies, Jess. I was raised to believe that adultery is a sin. We're both living in sin."

"Please don't get upset," Jess said in a low voice. "I can't live without you. Can you live without me? It has to be one way or the other right now."

The shoppers had thinned out. Looking out a large glass window in the mall they could see the storm was getting worst with a heavy downpour and dark clouds. The wind was starting to blow hard.

"Maybe we should find a good place to eat," Jess told her, and Maggie nodded her approval.

"It's a good thing the car wasn't too far away," Maggie said, as they both hurried into it. But they were still soaked on their outer rain coats.

Jess turned Maggie's wet face toward him. "You didn't answer me back there. Could you live without me?" he asked.

"Darling, without you there would be no hope of tomorrow. I stay in a depressed worried state of mind because of our situation. But after knowing your love, I could never go on without you."

"Thanks, I needed to hear that from you." He kissed her on the tip of the nose and than each eyelid, slowly moving his lips down her cheek and onto her waiting lips.

She loved the way he caressed her—the special attention he lavished on her. She was sure he must be the best lover in the world. His tongue circled hers and she could feel his passion mounting as her longing for him heightened. She got a grip on her emotions and pulled away, moving to the other side of the seat.

"Jess, we're still in the car, remember? In front of a mall, where people are walking around," she kidded in a loving way.

"I know. I just can't wait to make love to you. It's been a long time. I don't know if I can last through dinner, touching you and not being able to grab you and make passionate love to you," He teased, pulling her to him kissing the tip of her nose then he turned his attention to the car in the heavy down pour of rain. She knew his moment of sensuality had passed, and he was once again in complete control.

They dashed inside the large restaurant from the parking lot. It was an Italian restaurant called the Courtyard. The entire building circled a huge court yard in a horseshoe design. The waiter asked if they prefer to sit by a window overlooking the yard. It was fascinating watching the storm from inside. The lightening crackled across the dark sky in waves of magic captivating it's audience, while the loud thunder reached out like shots from a cannon even through the thick windows of the restaurant. In the lighted court yard Spruce trees decorated with Christmas lights circled the huge pond throwing off crystal images in the water. The wind was whipping the trees causing the lights to shimmer even more

"That wind is getting pretty bad, Maggie, do you think maybe we should go back home after dinner?" Jess asked.

Maggie looked up at him with disappointment on her face. "Jess, after your scene in the car earlier, do you really mean that?" she asked.

"No, but I don't want you to be frightened. Sometimes these wind storms get worst through the night."

"Well, I want to be with you. We'll weather the storm together," she said.

They talked about what their children were doing through dinner, about the clothing shop and the animal clinic. Not being together for several months they had a lot of things to talk about.

"What about Julio's wife and kids? Does Angelina still work for you?" Jess asked.

"Oh yes, Angelina has become a very good seamtress. She's one of my best, and speaks almost fluent English now. The two oldest daughters went to college. One is working with a computer company and the other is a dental hygienist. Richard, the oldest son went into the service after high school, and the youngest three are still in high school I believe."

"I'm glad their lives turned out this way," Jess told her. "It was because of you it turned out so well."

"Things do happen for a reason, don't they? If Hueleo wouldn't have caused me a lot of grief, I may not have helped his family. May not have even thought of it."

CHAPTER 10

When they reached the motel Jess opened the trunk of his car and pulled out a small Christmas tree and lights to decorate it with. Maggie carried in a small suitcase where inside their room she took out two red candles in holders, a bottle of wine, a cheese ball, crackers and a container of her homemade cookies and candy.

"Well, looks like we're celebrating Christmas," Jess said as he turned Christmas music on the radio in the room

"Look what else I brought," Maggie told him as she held up a short black lace nightie.

"Now we're really celebrating," Jess said, as he took her in his arms and they danced to the soft music. He pulled her jacket off and drew her close massaging her back underneath her silk blouse.

"I've waited for weeks to be with you," he told her. "To hold you and make love to you so tenderly that you would never guess the wild passion that's underneath."

"Jess, you know I love your wild passion," Maggie laugh. "And I also love your tenderness."

"Which will it be Mame? Wild passion or mild tenderness?" He smiled at her. She loved him to tease and liked the twinkle of mischief in his eyes which turned to a serious gleam, as he pulled her close possessing her lips in a pursuit of heated desire which blotted out time, their unhappy marriages and any consequences which could accrue from their affair.

Maggie raised up on her elbow and watched Jess who had fallen asleep after their love making. He must be completely wore out she thought as she kissed him gently on his forehead. She hated to miss this time with him, but just being near him was paradise, after six months apart. She lay there and though about Adrian and Bill, wishing it could be different for all of them. She let him sleep for half an hour, but than couldn't resist waking him with a quick kiss on the lips. He stretched and pulled her close.

"I'm sorry I fall asleep. I don't want to miss out on one moment of being with you," he told her. "How long did I sleep?"

"A half an hour. You must be exhausted. We have the rest of the night together, Jess. Just hold me for awhile and than you can go back to sleep."

"It's more important that I'm with you than to sleep. I can always sleep, but I can't always have you beside me. Darling, I love you so much. I just feel like shouting it to everyone."

"I know. I feel the same way. Maybe someday we can. But right now let's decorate this Christmas tree and than I want you to open your present," Maggie told him, as she slipped back into her nightgown.

Jess put his underclothes on and pulled his pants on too. "All I brought is the colored lights to put on the tree," he said and started to weave the strand of lights around the small tree.

Maggie had already lit the candles when they first arrived. "That's all we need when the lights in here are off." She moved the candles from the dresser to the coffee table and took a beautiful wrapped present out of her suitcase.

When Jess had finished the tree she turned the lamp on by the bed and the main lights off. "Oh, Jess, what a beautiful tree. That was so thoughtful of you to bring it. Now here's your present. I hope you like it almost as much as I love my necklace."

Jess turned the small present, with the huge bow on top, around looking at it. "It's almost too pretty to unwrap," he noted as he untied the bow. "Oh Babe, their beautiful," he said as he looked at the solid gold cuff links with a small ruby stone in each one. He pulled her to him and kissed her. I love you. Merry Christmas."

"Merry Christmas, Darling," she answered.

They sat quietly watching the lights sparkle on the tree and holding each other for what seemed a long time.

"Did I see you bring some homemade cookies and candy in here?" Jess asked, looking around the room.

He poured them each a small glass of wine while she put the cheese ball and crackers along with some of her cookies and candy on a dish for them to nibble on.

"I thought maybe you could take what's left here back to the office for the staff to eat. I brought way too much for us to eat," she told him.

"Oh, they'll love this homemade stuff," he answered, while nibbling on a frosted sugar cookie.

"Maggie, do you want me to deliver your Christmas basket this year? You haven't mentioned it yet, so thought I better ask you."

"Yes, I'll have it ready two days before Christmas if you will pick it up at the house. I won't be there, but I'll tell Zelma that you will be coming to get it and she'll help you get it all to the car. I really appreciate you delivering it for me."

"Well, it's the least I can do. Where does it go this year?"

"A couple of my employees have been telling me about this new family in their neighborhood that's having a hard time. The husband recently broke his leg and the wife had to go to work waitressing because she has no work experience in anything, and they have five children at home. I told my employees that I would like to send the family food and gifts for Christmas and they all want to go in twenty dollars a piece to help buy the gifts. I didn't tell them I send the basket and gifts to a family every year. Christmas is getting kind of expensive. I'm giving all my employees a bonus plus a turkey this year."

"Could I add a hundred dollars to help out for the family?" Jess asked.

"Oh yes, that would be wonderful," Maggie told him.

"Wait, I have a better idea. Do you know how old the kids are?' He asked more enthusiastically.

"No, but I need to find out before I go shopping for toys. Sara said she would find out discreetly."

"I'll buy each one a new bicycle or tricycle or a little car to ride in depending on their ages. I'll have them delivered to their home. Would you mind if I do that?' He asked, as if maybe Maggie wouldn't want him to horn in so much.

"I think that would be great, Jess. Do you want to spend that much? Bicycles cost ."

"If it makes a kid happy for Christmas what the heck. I was poor at one time. My folks didn't have a lot while I was growing up. I went to college mostly on scholarships and part time jobs, so if it will make some kids happy at Christmas I would like to do it."

"Okay, as soon as I get the ages I'll let you know," Maggie told him, while nibbling on a cracker with cheese. "Now how did your thanksgiving turn out. Did the relatives all come?"

"Oh yeah! Adrian insisted on having it at our home this year. It did go quite well though. Adrian didn't throw any of her little tantrums. Her brother and his wife flew in from Arizona and stayed about three days, and Cris and his wife and the two grandchildren were there plus my mother and Adrian's parents."

"We had a nice time. Zelma and I gave Jonathan and his new wife cooking lessons the whole three days they were there. Apparently Lorie never was taught how to cook, and the poor kids were spending all their money eating out. So we had enough time to teach them some basic cooking methods."

"How are your parents doing?"

"Oh, they complain about the usual aches and pains that older people have, but I think they're doing well for their age. They miss Rosebriar. I should have them come visit more often, but I just don't have time with the business in town now. My dad told Bill that Rosebriar looks better than he has ever seen it look before. Well, Bill beamed. I could tell that he was thrilled for my dad to tell him that. Jess, I could never take it away from Bill. It's his whole life."

Jess pulled Maggie closer to him on the sofa. She laid her head on his shoulders and he tightened his arm around her. "How did Rosebriar get it's name?" he asked.

"From my grandparents. They built it. Let me tell you about how they met. It's a beautiful love story. My grandmother, Annie, was the youngest of five children. She was only two years old when her mother died giving birth to a baby boy that also died. Annie's maternal grandmother came to live with them in Missouri and take care of them, and lived until Annie was twelve years old."

"Well Annie's grandmother wrote to a distant relative named Christina that lived in Kansas. When her grandmother died Annie continued writing to Christina. When Christina was sick at a period in her life she had her son, Otto, write a letter to Annie, who was a beautiful young women by than. Their letters continued to each other and they fall in love through their writing. They decided to meet in person at the Kansas City train Depot in Leavenworth. Annie's older brother, Adolph, drove her there in a horse and buggy. So that they would know each other, Annie wore a hat with flowers on it and Otto wore a red rose in his suit lapel and a top hat which he wore a lot. They were both quiet dressy people."

"Well, I suppose they liked each other because they kept writing and Otto came to visit her and her family. One time when he came Annie was upstairs dressing when she heard a loud thump down stairs and ran down in her slip to see what the noise was. It was her dad and Otto that had come in the house, and while Otto was hanging his stove pipe hat it fell off the hat rack. She ran back upstairs but not before Otto had seen her in her slip."

They were later married in Kansas City and moved to Otto's home in Missouri. He had recently bought a farm there and didn't know the well water was contaminated. Annie caught Typhoid Fever from the water. Otto's sister and her husband, who live in town, came out to help take care of her. They traveled back and forth from town to the farm on a 'hand car' on the railroad. Do you know what a hand car is, Jess?" she asked.

"I've heard of them," was his answer.

"Well, it's on the railroad track, and they stood on it and pumped the handle bars someway to go down the track when they knew a train was not coming through."

"How did they know if a train was coming?" Asked Jess.

"I have no clue. But anyway, Annie was much better and they decided to move to Oklahoma which was still a territory and land could be homesteaded. They had a new covered wagon with a team of horses and old Shep, their dog."

Maggie took a sip of wine from her glass. "They accumulated a lot of land and cattle, but friends in Colorado kept urging them to move there when Annie wasn't gaining her health like she should. The friends said Colorado was a place where she would get well. So Annie rode on a passenger train to Colorado and Otto and Shep rode with their cattle in a freight train."

"Annie was so sick on the trip that an elderly man took her under his wing and gave her food and water and helped her off at the depot, staying with her until her friends came. Her and Otto settled on a ranch near Kingsburg."

"A year later a son was born to them and than a daughter, which was my mother. They lived in a dug out on the prairie which was said to be cool in the summer and warm in the winter. But their problems were still not over because their son had leakage of the heart and the doctors told them to move to a lower climate. So they moved back to Missouri in a Motel T with side curtains. They spent the nights in camp grounds where there was water and toilets. They arrived in Jasper, Missouri and stayed in a hotel for a week or so until they bought ten acres with a house and barn on Highway 71. By this time the kids were in school and walked a quarter of a mile to a one room school house. It seems like hard luck was still punishing them, as their two story home burned completely to the ground and had to be rebuilt. Than my mother, their daughter, contacted Polio when she was fifteen. A few years later after she was completely healed from this except for a limp, they moved to California during the years of the dust bowl in the middle united states. That was during the depression."

"Well, they bought twenty acres where Rosebriar is now and built that home and bought more land and cattle every year. They had a hard life before and Rosebriar met so much to them because they were blessed with good health and financial status after moving here. I was born and raised on that ranch."

"I can see why you can't give it up. That was a beautiful but sometimes sad life that your grandparents had. Kind of like ours. We're happy but sad too."

"That's what Rosebriar means," Maggie told him as she handed him a cracker with cheese on it. "Rose is for the happiness and briar is for the sadness."

The next morning they woke up early. The storm was still raging outside, but was much calmer than it had been through the night.

"Are you hungry?" Jess asked, propped up on two pillow in bed.

"Starved," Maggie answered. "I suppose we should get dressed and get an early start home, as much as I hate too."

"I know. How will I get along without seeing you for six more months. It's so hard, Maggie. It's like pulling my heart out to leave you."

Christmas music was playing on the radio. Jess pulled Maggie against him and kissed her lightly on the lips. The Christmas tree lights had stayed on all night and shimmered in the sunlight through the window.

"Oh, I have something else to give you, Jess, before I forget," Maggie told him and jumped out of bed to retrieve an envelope from her purse on the dresser. "It's a Christmas card and a letter. But please don't look at it until I leave you, and than whenever you miss me you can read it. And oh, my picture is in it too." Maggie continued, while placing the card in Jess's coat pocket.

"Thank you, Darling, I brought you a picture of me also that you requested," he told her.

"Well, at least we can look at each others picture and talk on the phone once in a while," Maggie said. "Jess, please don't let anyone get a hold of that letter. Keep it locked in your private safe."

"Where shall we meet in six months?" asked Jess.

"Why don't we drive up the north coast to the artist colony of Mendocino. It's peaceful there through the week days, and we could picnic on the beach and swim in the ocean and go to some art galleries."

"Sounds like Heaven," answered Jess. "Okay, it's set. I'll really be looking forward to it. Maggie, take care of yourself while we're apart. God, I don't know what I would do if something happened to you or you changed your mind about us."

"Darling, I'll never stop loving you, but sometimes I feel like telling Bill about us. I just feel like I can't go on deceiving him. And Adrian, we're cheating on her too."

"Maybe we should tell them both and get it over with. I know it would really hurt them for awhile, but they would get over it," Jess said assuredly.

"Yes, they would get over it. People would sure talk though. Do you think it would hurt our businesses?" Asked Maggie.

"Maybe for awhile. But people forget after a time and things would turn back to normal."

"Jess, we won't see each other for six months, until June, maybe we should wait till the six months is almost up before we tell them. Maybe something will happened in that time."

"I think you're right. No need to rush it," he answered.

"I'll always remember this Christmas with you as special," she told him, putting her arms around his neck and snuggling close.

CHAPTER 11

Maggie laid her paint brush down and moved back a few steps to examine the canvas. She glanced toward the nearby mountains. Returning again to the painting she added more green to the trees. She had not done any oil painting for two years, and wanted to get into the feel of it before her and Jess went to the art galleries in Mendocino next month.

The shrill ring of the phone tore at Maggie as she hurriedly added a touch of paint on the canvas. She would discourage the caller, who ever it was, from talking as soon as possible, so that she could return to her oil painting on the upstairs veranda. The door from the veranda led into her bedroom and she picked up the phone while sitting down into a green Queen Ann chair by the night stand.

"Hello".

"Maggie," the voice on the other end was almost as shrill as the ringing phone had been.

"Yes, this is Maggie."

The person on the phone was silent for several moments. "Stay away from my husband, you cheap fluzzy. I'm crippled, Can't you understand, I'm crippled. I have to hold on to him whether he loves me or not. He does love me, he just wants you for what he can get. No other reason, Maggie. Now stay out of his life. You'll never get him. Do you hear me, never, never. If you try to see him again I'll ruin your name and your business, and tell the whole country what their almighty veterinarian has done."

The phone went silent before Maggie could say anything. She slowly replaced it on it's cradle, stunned by her abrupt caller. Jess's wife knew, but how could she know. Maggie had not seen Jess for almost six months. Since last Christmas.

She pitied Adrian. Not only because of her being crippled, but because Adrian must know Jess no longer loved her. She had let her selfishness and self pity control her whole life. Maybe she wouldn't have lost Jess's love otherwise. Maggie picked the phone up again and dialed a number.

"May I speak to Dr Morgan, please."

"Yes, if you can hold for several minutes."

"Hello," came the familiar voice, "Dr. Morgan speaking."

"Jess, how are you?" Maggie asked. Her voice was shaky, but it felt good to hear him.

"Maggie, Hey, it's good to hear from you, Lady."

They were both silent. "Is something wrong, Maggie?"

"Are you alone in your office, Jess?" She asked.

"Yes."

"Can anyone listen in?"

"No, I have a private line. Maggie, what's wrong."

"Adrian just called me, Jess. She knows about us," Maggie said, with concern .

"My God! How did she find out?" Jess asked.

"I don't know. She just blurted out a bunch of words and hung up. I didn't get a chance to talk to her."

"Wait a minute, let me check my keys," he told her and left the phone. "The key to my private safe is missing off my key ring. She must have taken the key last night when I was sleeping and got into the safe and found your letter. I didn't want her to find out like this. I wanted to try to tell her about us gently. Well as gently as possible."

95

"Jess, you better go home to her and try to console her. She was very upset. I don't know what to do," Maggie said helplessly. "Should I call her. Jess, maybe you should just tell her it's over between us until we can work something out."

"But I don't want to lie to her," he said. "You don't think she would try suicide, do you?"

"Oh, I hope not. You better go to her, Jess, right away."

"Maggie, I'm so sorry this happened. She's never got into my safe before. She must have suspected something," he told her with anxiety clear in his voice. "Maggie, no matter what happens I love you very much. I'll get back to you."

"I'm sorry too, Jess. But just worry about Adrian for now. Take care of her. Do what you have to do to get her through this," she sadly told him.

Feeling heavy-hearted Maggie returned to her oil painting. She could always think better and plan when she was busy doing something. She knew she had to end it with Jess. But how? What would she tell him. How could they live without each other. How could she go on each day knowing they could never be together. There would be nothing to look forward to without him. But the only right thing to do was to end it even if Adrian had not found out about them.

Maggie waited all evening for Jess to call her about his confrontation with Adrian, but he never called. Down deep inside Maggie wished he would ask Adrian for a divorce, but it wouldn't be right and she didn't know if she could live with that either. No they had to break it off for their own peace of mind.

Jess didn't call until he got to the office early the next morning.

"Maggie, thank Heavens I went home right away yesterday like you wanted me to, because Adrian was just getting ready to swallow a bottle of pills."

"Oh Jess, is she alright?"

"Yes, but she's terrified that I'll leave her. She was hysterical. I can't tell her yet that I'm leaving. We'll have to give her time."

"Jess, maybe we should just end it for now and try to get on with our lives. We can't go on like this, always waiting for something that may never come about."

"Maggie, I can't say let's end it, but let's let it ride for now."

"I appreciate you calling, Jess, and letting me know what happened. I have to get down to the shop I have something important to take care of there," she told him. Feeling nauseated she headed to the bathroom.

"I'll call you in a week or two. Please take care, Maggie."

That was the first time they had not told each other 'I love you' at the end of their phone conversation.

The time went by slow and Maggie tried to keep busy at the shop. Julie and Steve had separated, and Julie had moved back home to Rosebriar into her old bedroom. They had filed for divorce so Maggie knew it was serious. She didn't try to talk Julie into going back, because she knew the main issue was children, and knew how much Julie wanted a baby.

Having Julie back home help ease the pain of losing Jess, but Maggie missed him so. The memory of his face kept coming to her. The face she loved so much, with the deep set gray eyes that smiled back at her and the mouth that curved up on each corner when he was happy and teasing.

'Why did you make me fall in love with you, Jess,' she whispered. 'I didn't want to. I didn't want to. My life has been Heaven and Hell since that first time you kissed me. I have to forget you, but how, how?' Her world only half way existed without Jess, it seemed. She was only completely happy when she had been with him. Since they were apart the real world returned and the guilt feelings rushed in to be buried deep in the soul returning again and again.

Maggie tried to get back into her dress designing, but she couldn't concentrate. It had been almost a year since she had been with Jess, and she longed to see him. Even though she had made up her mind to forget him, she couldn't seem to do this. She laid her head on her desk. She felt so tired and low, depressed to a point that she wished she could sleep forever. Falling asleep she dreamed that Jess was calling out to her, but she couldn't find him.

"Maggie, Maggie, are you alright?"

She felt someone patting her back as she bolted into an upright position in her desk chair.

"Oh, Jennifer, I must have dozed off."

"Maggie, are you alright? It isn't like you to fall asleep in the afternoon."

"I haven't been feeling well lately. It's just some personal problem I have to resolve," she told Jennifer, while she straightened her drawings out on the desk.

"I'm sorry Maggie. Would it help to talk to someone. I'm always willing to listen to problems," Jennifer said, and put her arms around Maggie's shoulders hugging her.

"You are a very special friend, Jennifer, but I don't know if you would understand."

"Well, try me."

Maggie was silent as if trying to work up enough courage to blurt her problem out. She got up and walked around her small office concentrating on how to begin. She shut the office door so that the other employees couldn't hear.

"You have to promise not to tell another living soul," Maggie said, looking directly into Jennifer's eyes. She looked away, "No, I can't tell you. I can't make it part of your problem too. You have enough problems of your own. Why should I let you be hurt by my predicament that I got myself into."

"Hey, Maggie, I'm your friend. Let me help you with whatever it is. And I promise not to tell anyone."

Maggie paced again trying to work up the courage to tell Jennifer. "I've had an affair with a married man. A doctor. I haven't been with him for over a year now, but I miss him and still love him so much, I just can't forget him."

Jennifer hugged her close. "Oh Maggie, you are in trouble. How long did this affair last?" She asked, still holding onto Maggie.

"Well, it's been six years now since it first started. After the first year, we only met every six months, but his wife found a letter I had wrote him and she went into hysterics and almost committed suicide. If I told you who he is I'm sure you would understand more. We were going to tell his wife and Bill, but because of his wife, we decided it would be best if we try to forget each other."

"Oh Maggie, you poor thing."

"Jennifer, I love him so much, I can hardly stand it. I just want to die."

"Hey Maggie, you have so much to live for. Your children and grandchildren. Your business. Does Bill have any clue of this?" she asked.

"No, no Bill doesn't have the slightest idea. Jennifer, Bill and I never had a very good marriage. He loves the ranch though and I could never tell him to leave it. We both just sort of go our own way."

"But, do you love Bill? I mean if you don't, why are you still married to him?"

"I love Bill, but not the way a wife should love a husband. But I can't divorce him because of Rosebriar. My family gave us the home and a lot of the land when my dad became ill and retired, but Bill helped make the ranch what it is today. He has worked so hard on that ranch that I could never ask him to leave or I could never sell it," she quietly said.

"How much does this doctor mean to you?" Jennifer asked.

"Everything," answered Maggie. "But I know I have to forget him. We've sinned and we're guilty, and it's time to let go. But how, how do I do it?" she asked in despair.

"Now Maggie, you have to put yourself in first place. There are ways to get a divorce without losing your home. You and Bill could work it out. And this wife probably never intended on killing herself. It was probably a big bluff to break you up. Most people bluff to get their way, but never intend completing the threat."

"But we can't take that chance. And Jennifer, if you knew who she was you would see. You would understand why I have to forget him."

"All I'm saying is you have to look out for yourself. Do what makes you happy. Things usually work out in time."

Jess still called her from time to time. Usually once a month. He assured her of his love for her, but somehow Maggie felt they were drifting away from each other. She had seen him several times at the ranch within the year, when he had to doctor a sick calf, but they had not really been together for well over a year. She told herself that she would slowly forget him, but still her undying love for him consumed her well being. She put more hours into her work at the shop and still did some traveling to companies in Oakland and San Francisco. Julie usually went with her and was learning that part of the business. Although her expertise was in designing for the younger generation, and Maggie was turning more of the designing over to Julie now. Julie seemed to be happy living at home again and dated occasionally with no one in particular. Maggie and her did find time to go horseback riding on the ranch together once in awhile, and sometimes was joined by Jennifer.

Maggie put the pile of papers down she was working on as she answered the phone.

"Hi Maggie, how are you?"

"Fine Jess, how are you?" she asked and closed her office door.

"Well, I miss you so much. I have to get away from Adrian. I just can't live like this much longer. I really need to see you."

"Jess, I miss you too, but we made an agreement not to see each other for the time being."

"Agreements are made to be broken. Maggie, I just want to look at you and talk to you. Nothing more, I promise."

Maggie hesitated, "Oh Jess, I don't know. If we see each other it might make things that much harder."

"Please meet me just to talk ," he pleaded. "I have to go to Austin to check some horses at three o'clock tomorrow, could you meet me there at a coffee shop about four o'clock? Please Maggie."

"Jess, how can I refuse you? I know it's against my better judgement, but I desperately need to see you to."

"Great! Meet me at the coffee shop at Heritage Inn at four."

Austin was a small town about a half an hour from Wilcottville and about twice the size of Wilcottville. Maggie had an appointment with a customer for a fitting tomorrow afternoon, but she could change that to the morning. A warm sensation at the thought of seeing Jess encircled her. She thought of Bill and Adrian and the guilt returned, but she pushed it aside with a stronger need to see Jess.

It was four fifteen, and Maggie was impatiently waiting for Jess to meet her at the coffee shop. She glanced around at the nicely decorated restaurant. A lot of tropical plants and ferns were placed everywhere, giving you the idea that you could be eating in a serene restaurant in Hawaii. The evening crowd had not arrived yet and it was quiet and calm with only a few customers chatting to each other.

"May I join you Mame, or are you expecting someone else?" Jess boldly asked, as he grasp the back of her neck and shoulders. Messaging them lightly before he sit across from her.

"Well, I was hoping a tall good looking gentleman would pick me up, but I guess I could settle for you." They both laugh.

Jess took her hand and kissed it lightly. "Thanks for meeting me. I've missed you so much. My world isn't complete unless you're in it with me," he told her.

Maggie's eyes clouded, "Will we ever be together, Jess, all the time, forever."

"I promise you we will someday."

They sat quietly together for awhile just gazing into each others eyes and holding hands across the table. "You're as beautiful as ever," Jess finally said. "How are things going at home?"

"Oh, Julie is still living at home. She's taken over a lot of my work at the shop. I really enjoy her living at home, but I hope she does get married and has the children she wants so badly. Jonathan is very busy being an attorney , and he and Lorie have two children now. Two little boys."

"Well, two little boys. So you're a grandma twice over now."

"Yes, I love it. Only wish I could see them more. They live so far away."

"And what is Bill doing lately?"

"Bill is still as busy as ever on the ranch. I don't see him very much. Which I suppose is good."

They were quiet again for awhile until Maggie broke the silence. "How is your family?"

"Adrian is doing better. For awhile she questioned my every move, but she's eased up a little. She's a diabetic now and has to take shots everyday, which isn't helping her health condition, along with high blood pressure."

"I do feel sorry for her, Jess. She has so many problems, I guess we don't need to add to them."

"I know, but it's so hard staying with her, and knowing you're out there waiting for us to have a life together. Sometimes it's almost unbearable. That's why I had to see you just for a little while." Jess took a drink of his coffee they had ordered earlier. "Cris and his wife are divorced now, which didn't help Adrian's health any."

"Oh I'm sorry to hear about that. What about the children? They must be getting pretty big now."

"Yeah, the boy is ten and the girl is eight. They spend the weekends with Cris. He brings them over to see us almost every weekend for a few hours."

"I suppose Adrian enjoys that, as I know you do."

"Well, you know how fussy Adrian can be. Poor kids they can't touch hardly anything or make any messes. I'm really surprise they come over as much as they do," Jess confided in her.

"Would you like something to eat, Maggie?" She shook her head no. "Let's order a small salad," Jess added, as he summoned a waitress. "If I don't eat when I get home Adrian will throw a fit."

"Well my goodness, Jess, she really does have the upper hand lately, doesn't she? I've never seen you so passive toward her before."

"I suppose it's just easier to get along with her that way. I just block a lot of it out."

They both had a light salad while they continued discussing the dress shop and the veterinary clinic and going back to their families from time to time.

"I hate to leave, Maggie, but I have one more stop here in Austin at another horse ranch before I go back to Wilcottville," said Jess, and took her hand again kissing it gently.

"Well I can't believe we've been sitting here talking for two hours. That time sure went fast, as it always does when I'm with you," she smiled. "I'll walk to your truck with you."

He lightly kissed her on the lips, "I need you. Please keep on loving me," he told her as he got into his truck. She watched him drive away with tears in her eyes.

CHAPTER 12

The seasons passed through another year. Spring was attempting to lift it's head from the long winter's sleep. The yellow Daffodils and other early flowers were peeping out of the ground and the grass was starting to green. Maggie sat on the bench by the large pond near her home, listening to the frog's joyful sounds that spring had arrived. She had not heard from Jess for several months. She knew he was alright or she would have heard around town. They had not talked very often through the year and Maggie was wondering if Jess still felt the same about her.

As she sat reflecting upon her thoughts, she heard Bill call to her from the house. "Out here," she waved to him. "Come on out." Watching Bill walk the stretch of ground to the pond it dawned on her that they were both reaching their fifties. His walk was slower now she noticed, and the bounce he use to have in his tall lanky frame was not as noticeable any more. Their youth was gone. Maybe she really should forget Jess and try to make things work with Bill.

When he reached her he was slightly out of breath. "That walk from the house to the pond seems to get longer," he said, and sat down on the bench beside her.

"Yes, we're not getting any younger, Bill. It's getting to be an effort to do a lot of things that use to be so easy."

"Maggie, I need to seriously talk to you." He ran his hand through his thinning hair as though he didn't know how to start. "We just haven't got along to well for a long time. For around ten years now, maybe longer.

It seems like you try to avoid me and I know you're really busy, and I'm busy with the cattle and everything, but I need something more." He hesitated awhile and Maggie started to speak, but he spoke first. "I need more companionship now. I don't know how to tell you this, Maggie, to make it easy, but I'm going to move away. I'll still take care of the cattle and orchards, but I have to go."

Maggie started to speak again, but Bill stopped her. "Let me finish, and then you can holler at me if you want. I've met a nice lady. She's a widow. You don't know her. Her and her husband bought the old Farrow place and moved here about three years ago. Than he died of a heart attack about eight months ago and I've been helping her some on her ranch. I met them both at the Farm Bureau meetings. She isn't pretty like you, and she's a little heavy set, but she needs me and I think I need her too. I'm truly sorry, Maggie. But there's been nothing between us for a long time. I've felt at times that you must love someone else, but I didn't want to know. I still don't want to know. I just think we should try to be happy in the years we have left to live."

"No, Bill, we haven't been happy. And I truly want you to be. I'm sorry I neglected you for so many years. And it is time for us both to be happy for the rest of our lives. You and, what is her name, Bill?" she asked.

"Lilly Pritchard," he answered.

"You and Lilly deserve to be together."

"Thank you. I'm glad this is okay with you, because I sure didn't want to argue about it. I'll get the divorce started right away. I'll probably rent an apartment in town until the divorce is final and we can get married."

"Bill, you don't have to move out. You can live here until you get married," she added.

"No, I think it's best I move out. I'll be back everyday to take care of things. We'll have to discuss later the business part of the ranch, but I don't think this is the time to discuss that. Not right now anyway. Thank you, Maggie, for understanding," he said, as he hugged her and kissed her on the forehead as they both stood. "I'm going to go pack a few things , just what I need for now," he said, and walked back toward the house.

Maggie sat back down heavy hearted, but yet glad her marriage was finally ending . She was free to marry Jess. But he wasn't free to marry her. And maybe he didn't even really want her anymore. She hadn't told Bill about Jess, because he indicated he didn't really want to know if there was someone else in her life. Well, there wasn't now. She was alone. What would she do with the rest of her life. What would they tell the kids about their father moving out and getting married? The truth she supposed would be best.

Jonathan took his dad moving out of the house very hard. He protested to both Bill and Maggie about getting a divorce, but Julie convinced him that it was for the best. That mom and dad no longer loved each other and needed to get on with their lives in another direction.

Julie wanted Maggie to go on a trip with her to Hawaii. She kept pestering her mother until Maggie finally said she would think about it.

"It would really be good for you, Mom, to get away for awhile," she told her. "You need a vacation. You could rest and it would be so much fun to go together."

"Well, okay, you make the flight arrangements and the motel reservations, and I'll see that everything will be taken care of at the shop while we're gone," Maggie told her. "Better call your father and tell him just in case he would need us, and Jonathan too. I'll tell Zelma. There's no need for her to work when there won't be anyone here to cook for or clean up after. Maybe she'll want to go stay with her daughter for a few days.

That evening Julie called to tell Maggie there had been a change of plans. "I hope you won't mind, Mother, that I changed our plans, but this trip to New Orleans for the Mardi Gras sounded like so much fun, I took the liberty of booking us with a tour group for that."

"Well, I've been to Hawaii before, so yeah, New Orleans sounds like a lot of fun,"

"Oh good, I'm glad you approve. We leave next Friday for eight days. I'm going to start getting my clothes ready. It may still be a little chilly there so pack some warm clothes too, but the travel agent thought it would be kind of hot there this time of year. I'm still at the office, but I'll be home in awhile."

Jess finally called her and she told him she was going on a trip with Julie. "I'm glad you're going with Julie, Maggie, you deserve to have some fun.

I'm still planning on taking that overseas trip with you someday," he told her.

"Jess, I haven't told you yet that Bill moved out. He's getting married. He met a lady and her husband at the Farm Bureau meetings, and her husband died of a heart attack about a year ago."

Jess was speechless. "He really moved out? Maggie, that's just one less obstacle for us to cross. Who is this lady?" He asked.

"Her name if Lilly Pritchard. They bought the old Farrow place."

"Oh yes, I've met her. I took care of a sick cow for her."

"Is she nice? Did you like her?" asked Maggie.

"Well yeah, I guess. She seemed friendly. She just wouldn't strike me as being Bill's type. He's tall and she's sort of short and plump."

"I guess it's what's in the heart that counts. Bill says she makes him feel needed. I suppose I did really neglect Bill the last ten years. You were always on my mind. I just couldn't think of anything else."

"Maggie, I would sure like to see you. Do you think we could get together when you get back from your trip? Just to talk, I promise, nothing else."

"Jess, I'll call you when I get back and we'll discuss it, okay?"

"Sounds good. Have a great time. I'll be thinking of you. I love you very much."

It was good to hear him say those words again. It had been a long time. "Oh Jess, I love you too. So very much.

Maggie and Julie met their tour group in San Francisco and enjoyed a get-acquainted dinner that evening at their motel. The next morning the group flew to New Orleans and were taken to their motel close to the French Quarter. That evening they had a champagne reception and dinner dance. Their group consisted of five ladies probably in their late sixties, Maggie guessed, that all seem to come together, and four couples from their thirties through their seventies, than several single young ladies more Julie's age, and several men from about forty to sixty years in age.

The next day they were taken on a tour to the French Quarter, Jackson Square, Farmer's Market, Lake Ponchartrain and the Louisiana Superdome. That evening, after resting in their rooms for an hour, they watched the Bacchus Parade of twenty four colorful floats and more than two hundred costumed participants, and caught beads that were thrown to them from the floats.

They had become acquainted with the other people in the group and knew most of them by their first name now. The next day they boarded a steamship and was taken on the Mississippi River cruise. That night they attended the dinner and festivities at the semi formal Mardi Gras Ball. Maggie and Julie both were exhausted from dancing almost every dance with some of the men in their group.

On "Fat Tuesday" they viewed the Zulu and Rex Parades. It was crowded and noisy, but added to the excitement of the famed celebration. The rest of their trip they visited old plantations and went to Baton Rouge visiting the State Capital Building. They dined on Cajun food and enjoyed the lively music and more dancing.

Maggie enjoyed the attention of two single men in their group who both seemed intent on doing all they could for her. It was fun for awhile, but she wished just her and Julie could have more time together away from the group.

"Mother, on the flight home could we please just sat together. I need to talk to you about something important."

After that, Maggie pondered over what could be so important that Julie wanted to talk about. She found out on the flight home when Julie told her she had been dating someone she really liked.

"I think you know him, Mother. His name is Cris Morgan."

"You mean our veterinarian, Dr. Morgan's son?" Maggie asked, in astonishment.

"Yes, Mother, Dr. Jess Morgan's son. He's been divorced for awhile now and I ran into him when I was out to lunch one day. We started talking and I found out who he was, and he remembered his dad had mentioned our ranch and our name before."

Maggie looked at her daughter. Her dark brown hair glistened in the sun that filtered through the small window of the airplane where they were seated. She looked a lot like her and Maggie could see her youth in her daughter.

"Have you been dating him long?"

"Well, at first it was just off and on for about six months, but now for two weeks we've been seeing a lot of each other. I think he really likes me, Mother, and I think I'm in love with him."

"Go slow, Julie, he has two children to support, you know. And if marriage is in the future for you, he may not want more children," Maggie told her, with concern in her voice.

" I know he does, Mother. We talked about kids and he wants at least two more he said. He loves children he told me. How did you know he had two children?"

"Oh, Dr. Morgan and I talk from time to time. He tells me about his family."

 Maggie felt guilty, and turned her eyes away from Julie, looking out the window. She wished she could tell her that her and Cris' father had loved each other for a long time, but now wasn't the time. Maybe someday she would have to tell her. But Julie and Cris, what would become of that. If they decided to get married Adrian would really flip.

"Do you know that Cris' mother is crippled and very hard to get along with?" she asked.

"Yes, he's told me about his mother. He loves her, but says she's moody and has temper tantrums a lot."

"This could be inherent in his children. In your children if you married him." She told Julie.

"Oh mother, don't be so dramatic. You act like you don't like Cris and you don't even know him."

"Julie, it's no fun to have a mother-in-law that's hard to get along with no matter how much you love her son."

"Mother stop worrying. We don't even know if we love each other enough to get married yet. Don't worry about it until there's something to worry about," Julie told her with annoyance in her voice.

"Alright, I won't say anymore. I'm sure Cris is a very good person. Just don't rush into something, Julie, Please," she told her and kissed her on the forehead.

"I think I'll sleep for awhile, Mother, I'm exhausted from this vacation," Julie laugh, "I wanted to get you away for a good rest, and instead we're more tired than before we started."

"Oh, we had a good time though. I could have lost a few pounds from all that dancing, but than I turned around and ate all that great food like there was no tomorrow," Maggie laugh at herself.

Julie nudged her and quietly said, "Mom, do you like any of these old guys in our tour group?"

Maggie smiled, to Julie, old was anyone over forty. "Yes, there are a couple of cute nice ones, but I'm not interested in anyone just yet. Now go to sleep. I probably will too."

She sat there thinking about what the future held for all of them. Things were changing fast all of a sudden. Bill was getting married and Julie was serious about someone. Jess wanted to get together with her when she returned. It had been a long time since she had felt his arms around her and his gentle passionate kisses on her lips. How she longed for him, but knew she should resist meeting him. She didn't feel as guilty if they just talked once in awhile, but if she slept with him the guilt would return, and she didn't think she could live with that again.

CHAPTER 13

Maggie delayed calling Jess when she returned from New Orleans. She knew he would want her to meet him, even though they had agreed not to be together intimately until they were both free. And they were only half free now that Bill had moved out of the house and filed for divorce, but there was still Adrian.

The large tub was filling with water and bubbles from the Vanilla Cream bubble bath. Maggie had left the shop early with a bad headache, and decided to relax in a hot tub with lit candles around the bathroom. Just as she started to get into the tub the phone rang. She put her white bath robe back on and hurried to the phone in the bedroom.

"Hello,"

"Hello, Maggie. Did you have a nice vacation?"

"Yes Jess, it was very nice. We had a lot of fun. We were wore out when we returned, and I went to get some rest," she laugh. "How are you doing?"

"Fine, but I was hoping you would call me when you returned."

"Jess, I know you want to get together, but I just think it's better if we don't. I just don't think I can go through being with you until you're completely free."

"Maggie, believe me I want to ask Adrian for a divorce, but she's worst physically. If I left her now it would probably cause her to have a stroke or heart attack." They were both silent for awhile. "Please, Maggie, I need to see you. I want to hold you and touch you, but I won't do that if that's what you're afraid of. I'll just look at you and hold your hand. I need to know you still love me."

"Jess, you know that I'll always love you no matter what happens. How could I ever forget you. You're my first thought in the morning and my last thought at night. Our love is beautiful and I'll always remember it that way" Maggie cried, as she hunted for a tissue, but I can't be with you while you still have a wife."

"Darling, I'm sorry. I'm so sorry for what I've put you through. It's okay. We don't have to meet now. As long as I know you still love me. You're like a life sustainer that's kept me going all these years. Without you I would be nothing, just a robot that works, eats, and sleeps. Just knowing I can call you on the phone and you'll be there keeps me going."

"Jess, you have a beautiful way with words. And I know you mean them. It's just that our life is passing us by and there isn't really anything we can do about it."

"You're free now to meet other men, Maggie. I won't hold you to anything if that is what you want."

"Don't be silly, Jess. You know that isn't what I want. Let's keep talking on the phone whenever we can and things will eventually work out," she told him.

Summer was coming to an end, and the trees in the orchard were turning into their brilliant fall colors. Bill was at the ranch most of the time now harvesting the apples and getting ready to harvest the walnuts soon. He and Maggie had worked out their business arrangement with both of them staying as partners on the orchards and cattle. Bill and Lilly had went to Lake Tahoe and got married as soon as the divorce was final.

Jess had kept to his word of not asking Maggie to meet him anymore. At times she felt she couldn't go on without being with him. They talked on the phone about once a month and he always told her she didn't have to wait for him, but she knew after knowing his love there could never be anyone else.

Maggie's eyes searched the familiar surroundings inside the church. She missed coming here----missed the presence of the Lord in her life. She gazed at the wooden cross on the wall behind the pulpit, with the replica of the Savior on it. Her eyes moistened, she whispered, "Please forgive me." She knelt at the altar and wept for sometime.

Finally she raised her eyes toward the cross, "Oh Lord, I love Jess so much, but I know I have to give him up. I have no right to love him like this. Please help me to forget him. To stop loving him as I do. To love him only as a friend."

Her faith in God had help pull her through hard times before, and she knew he would this time. She could feel his presence and knew he would silently help her in his own way. Even though she had sinned, Maggie's early religious training taught her she was still a child of God and asking forgiveness put her in his presence again.

Julie and Cris were still dating and it was looking serious to Maggie. Cris was a lot like his father, and Maggie enjoyed having Julie and him spend time at home on the weekends. Sometime he would bring his son and daughter and they would all watch movies and eat popcorn together in the family room with a fire roaring in the fireplace.

Jess had been very surprised when Maggie had told him last spring that Julie and Cris were dating. He seemed kind of happy that their family was joining in some way, and mentioned to Maggie that it would be nice if her daughter and his son decided to get married. All though they discussed how terrible Adrian would take it after their affair.

"I'm afraid she may be awful nasty to Julie, and Julie won't even know why," he had told Maggie. "I guess we've caused problems we didn't even think could happen."

"Mother, I'm sorry I'm late," Julie said, as she rushed into Maggie's office closing the door behind her, "Cris had the children all weekend, so he wanted me to meet him for breakfast this morning at the Tiffeny Inn. That's where I've been," she told Maggie all in one breath.

"Well, he's getting a little high classed," Maggie laugh, " taking you to breakfast at the Tiffeny Inn."

"Mother, look, look," Julie said ecstatically, as she extended her left arm out from behind her back displaying a beautiful diamond engagement ring on her finger. "What he did was so sweet. He had the waitress bring it out in a little covered dish. I thought it was the butter dish and when I opened it there the ring was on a small white satin pillow. His children even knew about it."

Maggie's mouth dropped open as she held her daughter's hand gazing at the ring. She pulled Julie into her arms, "I'm so happy for you and Cris. He's a wonderful man, Julie. I hope you'll be very happy with him."

"We were talking about wedding plans, Mother, and we would like to have the wedding in the yard at Rosebriar. Just a small wedding with only our families and a few close friends."

"Well, if that's what you both want than we should have it there. Have you sat a date?"

"We were thinking sometime around the first of May. That will give us time to get through the holidays and give us four months after that to plan it. Not that it will take a lot of planning for such a small wedding, but we can take our time and leisurely do it. And maybe Cris' mother will learn to like me more in the mean time," she told Maggie. "I don't know what it is with his mother. She acts like she just hates me and she doesn't even hardly know me. Is she jealous of me, Mother, or what?"

Maggie was sullen, "She'll come around after she sees what a wonderful person you really are," she told her. Maggie wished she could tell her daughter why Adrian was so resentful toward her, but she couldn't tell her yet. It could even ruin things between Julie and Cris. No, now wasn't yet the time.

"I'm so excited. Let's go tell Jennifer and the other employees the news, Mother."

"Fine, but first, Julie, I want to ask if you and Cris discussed where you will live? Since your father moved out and remarried, what about you and Cris living at Rosebriar? It's plenty big enough, and Zelma and I don't need all that room by ourselves. You could redecorate your bedroom for you and Cris, and refurnish Jonathan's room for the children, because they will probably be with you most weekends."

"I would love that, Mom, but I'll have to discuss it with Cris. He's so independent about things. He might feel like it would be taking advantage of you."

"But I would love it. It's so lonesome when you're not there," Maggie told her.

"As long as we're kind of on this same subject, Mother, I've been wanting to discuss something else with you. You know Cris doesn't really like his job, even though it's a great job with good pay and benefits, he wishes at times that he would have went to school to become a veterinarian like his dad, because he likes to work outdoors. I told him that dad could sure use a good man to take over most of the ranch work. He seems kind of interested. Do you think Dad would let Cris take over some?" She questioned Maggie.

"I noticed that your father is not getting around as good as he use to, and he also mentioned that he has arthritis now. If Cris really wants to give up his good job and take over some of the ranch after you're married I think you should talk to your father about it now."

Maggie walked toward the office door. Opening it, she beckon for Julie to go through it. "Let's go tell these ladies about the wonderful news."

Maggie sat down in the big leather recliner to read the Sacramento newspaper. It was Sunday evening and she was lonesome after being home alone all day. Zelma had went away for the day and Julie was spending time with Cris and the children on a fishing trip. She heard the back door open and shut and recognized Julie's footsteps through the rooms.

"I'm in the family room, Julie."

Julie flung herself down in the other big chair, "I'm exhausted from the weekend. Thank Heaven tomorrow is Monday."

"How was the fishing trip?" Maggie asked, still looking at the paper.

"Oh, it was fun, but we walked for half a mile to get to this little fishing hole and then the kids were hungry. So we got our lines in the water and ate our fried chicken lunch with dirty hands. And Zack got sick from putting the worms on his hook and threw up his lunch, and his dog got tangled up in his fishing line.

"Well, that's what kids are about. Did you catch any fish?' Maggie asked, laying down the newspaper.

"We all caught some and Cris is going to grill them for us next weekend. But Mother, we had a dreadful time Saturday night. We invited Cris' parents out for dinner to tell them about our engagement. Well Cris practically had to beg his mother before she would consent to come. And then I thought she was going to throw a little hissy right there in the Tiffeny Inn when Cris told them we were engaged. She turned white, Mother, and then she turned red, and we thought she was going to die right there. I'm thankful Mr. Morgan is a doctor and got her calmed down or I think she may have. Than she wouldn't look me directly in the eyes the rest of the evening. Just looked at her plate and picked at her food, sulking. What is wrong with the women. She acts like I'm a street walker."

"I'm sorry, Julie. Maybe it's not even you she's upset about. Maybe it's something else," Maggie told her with concern. "Adrian has always been very difficult to get along with. In the women's club we both belong to she always has to have her way about everything. And usually the other women let her get away with it. She has a controlling way about her, and I think she uses her paralysis to get away with it too. Jess, Dr. Morgan, told me once that she threw a hot bowl of soup at her nurse, burning her and causing the nurse to go into shock. He happened to be there and took care of the situation, but he was afraid that the nurse might sue them. I guess nothing ever became of it. He said it really did scare Adrian though and he thought she learned a lesson from it."

"Well, Dr. Morgan, bless his heart. He is so sweet to me. I think it's because his wife is so hateful, but I think he really does like me and is pleased with the engagement," Julie told her.

Maggie smiled, pleased at knowing that. She hadn't talked to Jess for awhile. Not since long before the engagement news. Christmas was coming up and that was one of their most important times to be together. But it wouldn't be this year or any other year in the future now. She didn't know what she would do with the rest of her life. But she did know she could never love anyone again after Jess. Now she had to concentrate on how to get them all through this wedding without upsetting Adrian and everyone else. What is the old saying she thought, 'Oh what terrible webs we weave'. Something like that.

The evenings were turning cold. Christmas was only two weeks away, and a light snow was predicted in the foothills of California. They had a long Indian summer, through Thanksgiving and into December. Maggie appreciated the nice weather because she took more time now to go horseback riding and do her oil painting down by the pond. But the cold weather brought the hint of Christmas in the air, and snow for the holiday would be wonderful. She often wondered how it could feel like Christmas in the warm climates of the world.

Maggie had most of her Christmas shopping finished and had decorated her home, mostly for Cris's children she told herself. And of course Jonathan and his family would be there for several days at Christmas. Jonathan had finally got over his indifference with his father for leaving home, and they had spent Thanksgiving day with Bill and Lilly.

Cris was going to cut the Christmas tree that Maggie had picked out on their property, and they were going to decorate it this weekend when his children came to visit. Maggie did enjoy Cris' son and daughter, and they spent most of the weekends at Rosebriar. Julie and Cris had agreed to live at Rosebriar after they were married in May. Bill was also going to let Cris take over a lot of his work at the ranch, and had started training him on the weekends for the orchard care and also what needed to be done with the cattle through the year. Bill would be there part time, but he also had Lilly's small ranch to take of.

Jess called to say he would deliver the Christmas basket again this year and asked who was getting it, and if he could help with the toys.

"Of course you can help with the toys," Maggie told him. And the basket is going to a family here, the Flannigans, whose home just burned completely down and they lost everything."

"Yes, I heard about that fire. They were lucky to all get out alive I also heard."

"Well Jess, they have four children. A daughter five years old, and three sons, ages three, six and eight. Any toys you can get for them would really be appreciated. Christmas sure is getting expensive now with bonus to all the employees and four children in our family now. I over did it this year buying things for Jonathan's boys and your two grandchildren. I had so much fun shopping for them, but I know I bought too much. Julie and Cris are going to have a fit and tell me I'm spoiling them," Maggie giggled.

"I wish I could have seen you shopping and playing with the toys in the stores," he told her. "Better yet, I wish I could have been with you shopping. Maybe someday it will happen."

Maggie changed the subject. "After the holidays are over we're going to start planning the wedding. It will be small. Just our families and the employees at the shop, and a few of Julie and Cris' best friends."

"I'm glad they just want a small wedding. Your yard will be a beautiful place to have it. I hope everything will go well with our families," Jess said, with a worried note in his voice.

"Is Adrian taken this all okay?" Maggie asked.

"You really don't want to know," Jess answered. "She's very jealous that they want to have the wedding in your yard, but hasn't said anything to Cris. She'll get over it. I just hope she doesn't make a scene during the reception. She knows that Bill remarried and of course she's worried that you and I may get together again."

"Oh I hope she doesn't make a scene. What if she says something about us, Jess?"

"I'm warning her ahead of time not to say anything. This is Julie and Cris' wedding day. She surely won't ruin it for them. I just hope she keeps a level head that day. So are the kids all coming over for Christmas dinner?"

"Yes, and my parents too. We'll miss Bill's parents this year, but I'm sure they'll be going to Bill and Lillys. I'm trying to stay friends with Bill's family, but I know they're upset with both Bill and I over the divorce."

"Well, sometimes it just takes time to work out," Jess answered.

"What will you and Adrian be doing for Christmas?" She asked.

"Some of her family are coming over I think. I let her handle that. She's happier if she plans it and I don't interfere," Jess laugh.

"Well, I hope you have a good Christmas, Jess. You know I would love to be with you, but it's impossible now."

"And you know, Maggie, how very much I want to be with you, but I know we can't. We have some good memories together at Christmas. I'll dwell on those for now."

Jonathan, Lorie and their two boys arrived early Christmas morning At Rosebriar. Cris and his children followed. Everyone was anxious to open their Christmas presents and settled down in the family room with a fire roaring in the fireplace; the tree lit with beautiful rainbow colored lights and decorations; and gifts piled high underneath.

Maggie asked Jonathan if he would pass the gifts out, and the children anxiously opened their gifts with excitement. Afterwards they sang Christmas songs and Maggie read the story in the Bible of the birth of Christ, before they sat down to a brunch that Maggie and Zelma had made. French toast with strawberries and powder sugar on top was a favorite with the children, along with a selection of fruit and bacon and scrambled eggs.

The children had enough toys to keep them busy the rest of the morning while the women prepared the ham dinner. Lorie had become a pretty good cook, and was preparing her special sweet potato casserole and jello cottage cheese salad that was a favorite with everyone.

Jonathan and Cris were becoming better acquainted and found they both liked to fish and hunt and planned to get together during the nice weather for a fishing trip. The children played together and seemed to get along even though Cris' children were a few years older than Jonathan's boys.

Maggie's mother and father arrived early in the afternoon with more presents for everyone, which added to the children's excitement. They all sat down around two o'clock while Maggie's dad ask the blessing over the Christmas dinner.

The main topic at dinner was the upcoming wedding, and Cris learning to help run Rosebriar. Maggie's dad gave him a lot of pointers about the cattle, because this had been his main line of work, cattle ranching and farming. Cris understood the old man had a lot of knowledge in this and listened intensely. He also understood that he had helped his father-in-law build Rosebriar into the successful ranch that it was today, and he than taught

Bill to take over. The old man praised Cris' father and told him what a fine veterinarian his father was. This pleased Maggie to hear her own father saying great things about Jess. Things that she only knew too well.

"Well, we're certainly looking forward to this wedding and then some more grandchildren soon," Maggie's mother added.

"We're hoping to have at least two more children, grandma. Cris and I would like an even larger family, but I don't know if we can afford more. We want his children to stay with us on the weekends. It's so much fun at the holidays to have a big family," Julie told her grandma."

Everyone was just finishing their dinner when Julie exclaimed, "Oh look, kids, it's beginning to snow!"

The children hurried to the large picture window in the dinning room followed by the rest of the family, to watch the pure white flakes slowly drift to the ground covering it in a blanket of soft snow.

"Can we go out and play in it?" one of them ask.

"Yeah, can we, please," echoed the other three.

"Put your hats and coats on," Julie told them.

"And your gloves too," added Lorie.

"Oh, thank you, God, for letting it finally snow at Christmas," Cris' daughter said, while the family all laugh at her and clapped their hands in agreement.

CHAPTER 14

Maggie decided she should call Adrian and try to make amends with her on the phone before they met face to face at the wedding. She wanted to get along with Adrian and was trying very hard to forget Jess and only think of him as a friend. It had been easier, she had to admit, since she prayed at the church and had continued praying to forget him as a lover.

The nurse answered the phone and handed it to Adrian.

"This is Maggie, Adrian. I though perhaps we should talk to each other before the wedding."

"Well, what do you want?" She asked. "I'm very busy at the moment."

"I would just like for us to be friends again. I know what I did to you is very very hard to forgive, and I don't expect you to, but I wish we could just be on talking terms for the kids sake. I'm so sorry for what I did. There's no excuse, it just happened."

"Hold on for a moment," Adrian told her before Maggie heard her say to her nurse, "Can I please have some privacy while I'm on the phone." Maggie heard the nurse leave the room and shut the door. "I don't expect to ever be friends with you again. I'll come to the wedding just for Cris, nobody else, and I'll try my best to be civil to you, but don't expect me to be nice."

"Adrian, for Julie's sake, couldn't you just be a little nicer to her? She doesn't know why you don't like her. It isn't her fault for my mistake."

"She just reminds me of you and what you did with my husband. I don't really know if I can ever be nice to her. I want you to see your daughter hurt. I want you to suffer for what you did."

"Adrian, it's over between Jess and I. How can you be so cruel to the women your son loves and is going to marry? They want to have children right away. Are you going to treat their children bad, your grandchildren?" Maggie asked.

"I can't talk anymore. I have to take some medication," Adrian said rudely, and hung the phone up.

Maggie hoped Adrian would think about what she said and change a little bit for Julie's sake, but than it could make her worse. Well, Heaven help them at the wedding she thought.

It was a beautiful sunny day in May with a bright blue sky and a few fluffy white clouds hanging low. There had been a lot of rain showers in April, but May brought the warm sunny days. It was a perfect day for an outside wedding. The Weeping Cherry Trees and the Bradford Pear trees were all in full bloom, adding a magnificent appearance to the huge yard. Vast stone vases of Lilies, Dahlias and Fern were placed about, while two colossal kneeling cherubs holding up clear glass bowls of floating candles and roses graced the yard.

The guests were starting to arrive a little before the eleven o'clock wedding was to begin. It made quite a huge gathering with all of Julie and Cris' families, friends and some of the employees.

Bill introduced Lilly and her family to Jess and Adrian and the other family members that had not met yet, than excused himself to see if the bride was ready to start. Maggie had been busy helping Julie and her Maid of Honor get ready and slid into her chair as the music began. Bill walked the bride out on his arm and under an Ivy covered arch-way to her groom. He didn't look as nervous Maggie noticed, as he did at her first wedding, and thought it must be the familiarity of the yard.

Julie and Cris wrote their own vows, and some of it was so touching that you cold hear gasps and weeping from the audience at times. While the photographer took the family wedding pictures Zelma and some of Julie's girlfriends brought out large platters of finger food for the luncheon.

Maggie prayed she could get through the day with Jess so close, and Adrian following her every move. She didn't dare look directly at Jess because Adrian was always starring at her. As long as she had known Adrian she had always done most of the talking at the club meetings that they both attended, and any other gatherings. Now she sat there glaring, as though she were mad at the world. Jess stayed close to her, and Maggie knew he was afraid she would say something she shouldn't if he wasn't there.

Most of the older men were standing around talking in a group away from the table and chair area where the women were sitting. Jess finally walked over by the men to talk with them. Jennifer sat down next to Maggie telling her what a beautiful wedding it was.

"Where are the kids going on their honeymoon?" She asked.

"To Hawaii," Maggie answered.

"Oh! They'll have fun there," Jennifer commented. Turning to Adrian, she said, "so you and Maggie are in-laws now. We haven't seen you at the shop in a long time, Adrian, and you use to be one of our best customers. Have you been sick?"

"Yes," Adrian answered, "I don't get out very much anymore."

"Well, we can always bring items of clothing to your home to show you if you like," Jennifer told her.

Adrian didn't answer. The group of ladies continued talking about the growth of Wilcottville and the new shopping center being built.

One of the shop employees started telling about a customer that came in and bought about a thousand dollars worth of clothing, and the next day her husband brought all the clothing back and told them to close his wife's account. Said they were getting a divorce and he wouldn't be responsible for anymore of her bills.

" Oh, you mean that kind of young woman, Debbie what's her name. I heard she was having an affair with a married guy from the Lapco plant and that's why they're getting a divorce," one of the other shop employees spoke up.

Maggie sat there wondering why they had to bring something up like this in front of Adrian. She was glad the older women were sitting at another table and couldn't hear the gossip. She was about to change the subject when Adrian spoke up.

"The town ought to take a woman like that and string her up to a tree by her feet and leave her hang until she dies."

Everyone at the table was quiet. They were all just looking at Adrian. Maggie broke the silence as she rose and muttered she had to go check on the cake in the house. She hurried to the house and fled into the bathroom off the back entry. She sat in the bathroom for about ten minutes trying not to cry and mess up her makeup. There was a gentle knock on the door, and Maggie tightened up trying to think of an excuse to tell the intruder about her red eyes.

"Maggie, it's me, Jess."

She opened the door and Jess entered, locking the door behind him. "I saw you run to the house and knew Adrian must have said something."

"Jess, you shouldn't have followed."

"I know, I know. I just can't stand to see you hurt."

Maggie looked at him, seeing the love in his eyes for her, she reached for him and he enfolded her in his arms, holding her close as though he would never let her go. It had been so long since she had felt his arms around her. It made her feel secure and safe, but yet guilty.

"Oh Jess, I've been trying to forget you, but I still love you so," she whispered.

"Darling, I love you to, so much," he answered quietly, before his lips met hers with such passion that neither one of them wanted it to stop.

She pushed him gently away. No Jess, this kiss shouldn't have happened. We have no right."

"I know, I know," he answered.

"Okay, we have to compose ourselves before we go back out," Maggie said. "You go ahead and I'll bring the cake out in a little while. Go out the front door and around to the back." She straighten her hair and wiped her eyes with a tissue before she went out into the kitchen.

She looked at the three tier cake and decided she better have some help carrying it. Still shaking from being near Jess, she called Jennifer to come and help her. Jennifer came into the kitchen and looked kind of oddly at Maggie. Putting her arms around her she asked, "the man in the affair was Dr. Morgan, wasn't it Maggie? When Adrian said that, I put two and two together. I understand now why you said he couldn't leave her. But she's something else. I don't know how he lives with her. And I can see she would commit suicide, just to get even with you both if nothing else."

"I don't know how he lives with her either, Jennifer. He works long hours I think to keep his sanity. He's a good man. Most men wouldn't stay with a woman like that. Crippled and a nasty disposition too. Cris is so much like him. Nothing like Adrian. I only hope if Julie and him have children they're nothing like Adrian. Please don't tell anyone about Jess and I. It's over anyway."

"Are you sure about that? I can see you still got it bad for him. Isn't there something you can do?"

"No, no. Not now. Adrian's not in very good health. Sometimes I just wish she would die. No, I don't want to think like that. God help me, I don't want to have these feelings about her."

"Maggie, if you ever need someone to talk to about it, I'm always close by. And I promise I won't tell another living soul."

"Thank you, you're a good friend. I'll be okay, but I'm worried about the effects of this on Julie. Adrian is very hateful towards her and Julie doesn't know why. I called Adrian the other day to try to talk to her about Julie, and do you know what she told me?"

"Well, I can just about imagine," Jennifer answered.

"She said Julie reminded her of me and what I did with her husband. She said she wanted me to see Julie hurt. That she wanted me to suffer for what I did. I asked her how she could be so cruel to the women her son loved and was she going to treat their children that way?"

"What did she say to that?"

"Said she couldn't talk anymore, very rudely, and hung up on me."

"Poor Julie. Are you going to tell her about you and Jess?"

"Yes, when the time is right," she answered heavy-hearted. "Everything is so confusing. But I have to have faith that everything is going to be alright." She looked at her watch. "I better get back out in the yard. I've been in here way too long."

"Yes, let's go eat this beautiful cake," Jennifer laugh.

After the wedding presents were opened, the younger people and children danced on the brick terrace while the older generation talked and watched the dancing. Jess and Adrian left early saying she needed to go home and lay down. Jess' eyes had met Maggies for a moment before they left, and Maggie felt his love again, but turned away determined to forget him.

She knew she would have to tell Julie about their affair if Adrian kept being hateful, but she dreaded to. What would Julie think of her. And Cris. Julie would probably tell him. What would he think of both her and his father.

It was so lonesome while the kids were away on their honeymoon. The house seemed so big and quiet with only Maggie and the house keeper there. Maggie worked more hours at the shop and drove over to San Francisco one day to see clients there. The last client she visited asked if he could take her to a late lunch and she excepted.

It was a balmy day with a gentle breeze blowing. He picked a restaurant over looking the ocean and they decided to sat at a table with a large bay window. Several sailboats were off to a distant and they could see the sea lions on the rocks below. He ordered lobster and they ate until they could hardly get up. Maggie complemented him on choosing such a fine restaurant.

"This is the best seafood I've had in months," she told him. "You know we can hardly fine good lobster or crab at the restaurants in the foothills. It's really a treat to come over here."

"Well, you'll have to come more often, Maggie, now since you are divorced," he said to her in his slight Italian accent. "They have wonderful restaurants here. Anything you want.

"That was incredible, but now I'm in misery," she laugh.

"How about if we go dancing. That would make you feel better. I know of nice nightclub to go to."

Maggie studied Mario. He was nice looking with dark hair and eyes, just a little on the heavy side and looked to be about fifty. "Mario, you're married. What would your wife say,"

"Oh I go to this nightclub all time. Sometimes my wife goes and sometimes I go with other women. She don't care. We been married a long time."

"Well, thank you, Mario, but I fell in love with a married man once and I'll never do that again. I just don't date married men."

"Okay, I'll take you back to your car at the store."

It was just turning dark when they got back to the store and Mario walked Maggie to her car.

"Sure you won't change your mind about going out with me. We could make beautiful music together," he told her.

"No, Mario, but I really appreciate the wonderful late lunch we had. Thank you very much. And I'll ship the order of clothing to you in about three months."

"Fine," he said, before he grabbed Maggie and kissed her.

She didn't want to cause a scene or loose a big account so she let him kiss her before she got into her car and drove off. Still being kind of shook up at Mario's sudden kiss, she laugh at the silliness of it, and left San Francisco heading East thinking about Jess, remembering their few visits here in the bay area together. Their first night together was spent in San Francisco. She would love to relive that night and day spent with him. To feel the magic of their new love. The giddiness of their secret meeting. The selfishness they allowed themselves. But it only brought them heartache, and also to others. Maggie thought of the old saying 'it's better to have loved and lost, than never to have loved at all.' She didn't know if she could agree with that. It hurt an awful lot.

CHAPTER 15

Maggie gazed at herself in the dresser mirror. The years had been good to her. At fifty three she still had no visible wrinkles in her face, but her hair was starting to grey a little bit in the front. She had worn her hair short for the last several years, because she didn't think long hair looked appropriate on women over fifty.

She disrobed and checked her slender figure. Would Jess still like her body after all these years, she wondered. It had been so long since they had been together. His last kiss was at Julie and Cris' wedding. The memory of it still lingered in her mind and she had relived it many times. Sometimes she felt like she couldn't go on any longer without being near him, but the time went on. He dropped by Rosebriar from time to time to see Cris and Julie and sometimes Maggie was there, but their conversations were always casual. Adrian never left her home anymore, and her impertinent attitude toward Julie had never changed. Jess still called Maggie once in a while, about every other month, and she lived for these secret phone calls. He never pressured her about getting together anymore.

After the wedding Adrian had been so disrespectful to Julie that Maggie had to tell her about their affair. She hoped that the kids wouldn't turn against her and Jess. But she knew the animosity Adrian flung at Julie was killing her daughter inside. It was better they knew the truth than to go on not knowing why Adrian was so hateful. The day she had told Julie they had been home alone. Cris had went to a cattle auction with Bill.

"Mom, I knew you and Jess cared for each other," Julie told her. "I can see it in your eyes when you are together. You're both two beautiful loving people inside, and I don't disrespect you for loving him. I knew you and dad didn't have a real good marriage. And I can see how this could happen with Jess. He's a good person and needed someone like you with his marriage the way it was."

"Your Dad never knew. And since he's remarried I just as soon he never knew about it."

"Mom, I know I need to tell Cris because he's very upset at the way his mother treats me, but I don't see any need for anyone else to know. It will be our secret too. And maybe someday you and Jess can be together."

"Thank you, Julie. I'm so glad you understand. I only hope Cris will," she told her daughter and hugged her tight for a long time.

The children that Julie and Cris wanted so badly had not yet become a reality. They were beginning to talk of adoption and Maggie hoped they would adopt a child before they got much older. Maybe with the pressure off them to have a child, would help Julie to become pregnant. The medical tests they had both went through found no reason for Julie not to conceive.

Cris' son and daughter were now teenagers and spent most of their time with their friends on weekends instead of at Rosebriar like they did when they were younger. Maggie sure missed them and knew Jess also must miss seeing them more. She recalled the time the children had stayed over the weekend with her while Julie and Cris went to a clothing show in San Francisco. They had went fishing in the pond and had called grandpa Jess to come and fish to. Maggie knew nothing about Jess coming to fish, until he showed up with a basket of fried chicken from a restaurant in town, along with cold slaw and biscuits. She had made deviled eggs and a chocolate cake, so they had a feast on the old wooden table, that Maggie covered with a clean table cloth, next to the pond.

Jess told her that he had cancelled some of his appointments that day and had put as many as possible on his assistants. Since he had built the new clinic he had hired three more veterinarians to assist him because his practice had grown so much. He could take more time off now, but rarely did so.

They both had enjoyed that day fishing with the grandchildren. They all laugh together, and Jess and maggie's eyes met ever so often telling each other of their love, amidst the innocence of the grandchildren.

Julie and Cris were so happy even though there had been no baby yet. Cris' love for the ranch also grew. He added more cattle, and they purchased another hundred acres that had come up for sale next to their land. Bill still helped some at Rosebriar, but with his arthritis getting worse and all the work at Lilly's smaller ranch, Cris and hired hands did most of the work now.

Jonathan had opened his own law practice a few years back and even hired a young assistant to help him. He, Lorie and the two boys came to visit as often as they could from the city. Maggie wished many times they lived closer, but an attorney needed to be in a large city. She had missed so much of her grandson's growing up years, but she did get away to visit them more, now that Julie had taken over a lot of the clothing business for her.

Maggie slipped back into her robe, deciding to go back to bed and read a good book and maybe just stay in bed all day. She picked up a book she had recently purchased by one of her favorite authors, propped her pillows up and settled down to read. She was almost half way through the book when the phone rang.

"Mother, Adrian had a stroke and the ambulance took her to the hospital this morning. Cris has been with her and I suppose Jess too. I'm getting ready to leave the office and go to the hospital. I just thought you would want to know," Julie told her.

"I'm sorry to hear that," Maggie answered. "No, I'm not. Oh, Julie, I'm so confused. I don't want to dislike Adrian, but she has kept us apart for so long."

"I know, Mother. Maybe this is for the best. You and Jess need to be together. To get married and get on with your lives."

Maggie couldn't read anymore. She got up and dressed and went down stairs to fix a bite to eat. She called Jennifer at the store and talked awhile to her. Jennifer had already heard from Julie that Adrian was in the hospital.

"In her physical condition what does she have to live for?" Asked Jennifer. "Besides that, she's hateful to everyone I hear. She doesn't have any friends anymore."

"I don't know why I feel bad about her having a stroke, Jennifer, I guess because she's a human being," Maggie told her. "It was a terrible misfortune for her when they had that accident. You know it was Jess' fault, that's why he could never leave her after it. They were waiting for Cris to finish school before they got a divorce but the accident happened before."

"Do you think she had that terrible disposition before she was paralyzed?" Jennifer asked.

"Jess said she came from a well to do family and she was always spoiled and temperamental."

"Well see!" exclaimed Jennifer, "That's probably why the accident happened to her. What goes around comes around. If you do good things, that good comes back to you; but if you do bad things, bad comes back to you."

"Yes, there's a lot of truth in that, Jennifer, a lot."

They talked awhile longer and than Maggie tried to get back to reading her book. Late afternoon the phone rang. It was Julie asking if she felt like cooking dinner for them and Jess too. She said they didn't feel like going to a restaurant and they were all wore out and needed a shower and some rest before they went back to the hospital. Maggie looked in the refrigerator to see what she could find to cook. Zelma had made Lasagna for them yesterday before she left to go visit her daughter, but they had most of it for dinner last night and there wasn't enough left for four people. She did find a pound of lean ground beef and decided she would make Rigatoni with a tomato meat sauce and Ricotta. She hoped Julie and Cris would not mind having Italian food again tonight, but knew they loved it. With a tossed salad, garlic french bread and left over cheese cake that should make a complete dinner.

Cris and Julie came home first, saying Jess had went home to shower and change clothes, because he still had his medical clothes on when the hospital called him about Adrian. Julie helped Maggie finish the tossed salad and set the table . Jess arrived just as everything was ready to eat.

"I'm really sorry to hear about Adrian," Maggie told him.

"I know. It seems like she hasn't had much of a life for the last twenty years," he told them all.

Maggie knew he was blaming himself going back to the accident. "Jess, the car wreck was an accident. You didn't mean for it to happen. It's been a long time. You have to forgive yourself for that," she implied.

"Dad, we know it was an accident. You can't go on blaming yourself forever. It's time to get over it," Cris thoughtfully told his father. "Mom, didn't blame you for it, she knew."

Jess looked at his son in despair. " At times she did blame me. And I know her life would have been so much better if it wouldn't have happened."

"Well Dad, it happened and there is nothing we can do about it. Let's just concentrate on her now and what's best for her," Julie told him putting her arms around him. "Right now let's concentrate on this wonderful late lunch and get ready to go back to the hospital."

Jess seemed to calm down and enjoy lunch. "Maggie, this is the best meal I've had in months. Our housekeeper-cook doesn't cook very tasty food. I think she's a better housekeeper than she is a cook."

Maggie smiled, " She probably was taught to cook very bland food for people with health problems."

After dinner Julie and Cris went upstairs to shower and change clothes before going back to the hospital. Maggie assured them she didn't have anything to do and would clean the kitchen. Jess stayed for a little while visiting with her, but seemed tense and depressed.

"I hope she doesn't suffer anymore or goes into a coma," he told Maggie with concern in his voice. "It's unfair to her and to us to," he went on with his eyes focused on the floor. "I feel so helpless," he looked up at her and their eyes met. "I don't want her to suffer from the pain she goes through most of the time, and I don't want you to suffer from a broken heart."

"Jess, I'm alright for now. Don't worry about me. Just concentrate on Adrian. And take care of yourself. You look very tired and weary. Maybe you should take a week off from the clinic and rest while Adrian is in the hospital," Maggie told him affectionately.

"I suppose you're right. I do need a break and some rest. And I know my assistants can take care of everything," he said. He hesitated for awhile. I feel so distraught. We're getting older and I feel I wasted all our lives. I haven't loved Adrian for a long time and I should of filed for divorce years ago. I wasted those years; our years that we could have been together."

"But we both did it for Adrian. We couldn't have lived with ourselves otherwise," she wisely said. "We couldn't have been happy."

"I suppose you're right. It's just that I feel like I let you down most of the time, and myself as well. And Adrian too by letting her think that I loved her."

"Oh Jess, we can't dwell on what could have been. We did what we thought was best,"

Jess sat with his head lowered into his hand for a short time. "Well, I should get back to the hospital. I'll call you," he said, as he got up from the chair and kissed Maggie on the forehead before he left.

Adrian stayed in the care unit at the hospital for a month before she was able to come home. She had lost the use of her left arm from the stroke and her speech was impaired. Two nurses stayed with her, each in twelve hour shifts.

Maggie had not seen Jess since he had lunch with them, but he called and told her that he took a week off and rested up before returning to the clinic. Cris also told her that his father looked a lot more rested and was glad he had taken the time off.

The time went slow for Maggie. She did spend five to six hours a day at the shop doing various things. She still did some designing, but most of it was done by Julie now. She sewed on the clothing when she felt like it, and did all the bookkeeping and most of the ordering, but most of all she liked waiting on the customers. They always seemed so pleased with the new designs by Julie and Maggie, and the new styles coming in from other companies. Designs by Meg was still under contract with Roby International for a certain amount of designs each year. Julie and her made several trips a year to customers in the bay area and southern California. The company could have been much larger, but Maggie wanted to keep it small, small enough for just her and Julie to handle. Later if Julie wanted it to grow larger she could.

Julie and Cris had decided to adopt a six year old boy that needed a home. Bobby was very active. He was all boy. So once again Rosebriar was alive with laughter and the joy of a young child. Julie enrolled him into kindergarten at a private Christian school. When it was out at noon, he stayed there at a day care center, until Maggie picked him up after she left the shop to take him home with her. Maggie enjoyed spending time with him and he loved the huge yard of Rosebriar. Cris put a swing up for him on an old Oak tree where Julie and Jonathan had once had a swing.

Jess seemed to come by more often since Bobby came to live there. He took him fishing in the pond and bought him a Shetland Pony. Sometimes Maggie would join them at the pond or watch Bobby ride the pony in the corral with Jess instructing him.

Adrian never got over her hatefulness toward Julie and Julie finally quit going to see her with Cris. It hurt Julie, but hurt Maggie even more knowing she was the cause of it. Cris took Bobby to meet Adrian, but she ignored the boy so much that Cris never took him there again. Adrian's whole life consisted around Jess and Cris and the nurses that took care of her. The nurses never stayed over five or six months at a time due to Adrian's bad attitude. Jess finally got tired of interviewing for new nurses and just turned it over to a job agency.

He knew she suffered a lot which caused her to lash out at the nurses, and he talked to her trying to make her see why none of them stayed very long. She just couldn't seem to change her ways even though he knew she did try. He talked to Maggie about this problem, but it was something neither one of them knew what to do about it. There seemed to be no answer as far as Adrian changing.

Time went on and Adrian lived for several more years after she had the stroke. Maggie and Jess were both finally free to spend their lives together, but decided it would be best to wait four months before they announced they were getting married. Jess sold his home in town and purchased property in the country so that he and Maggie could keep their horses and do a lot of riding after they were married. They both decided to have a Spanish style home built on the property and designed the home themselves. Maggie knew she would miss Rosebriar having lived there all her life, but she would still be there a lot and knew it was in good hands with Cris and Julie.

Julie had finally become pregnant and was expecting in late summer. After waiting so long, the family was really excited about the new baby coming. Bobby, now eight years old, said he was old enough to help take of it and teach it to ride his pony he was outgrowing.

Cris' children were starting college. Jonathan and Lorie's sons were in high school. Maggie's father had passed away a year ago and her mother moved into a senior home. Maggie went to visit her as often as she could and brought her home to Rosebriar when ever her mother felt like it. Bill's parents had also passed away within the last four years. Nothing ever seemed to stay the same. The old pass away to make room for the new it seemed. It was sad, but it was life. Maggie knew her and Jess had lived most of their life. She was in her late fifties and he in his early sixties. With luck maybe they would have fifteen to twenty years together yet. When you're young it seems like you'll never get old, but looking back it seemed to have went so fast.

Maggie wanted to get married in church and Jess agreed. They would only have their immediate family there. Just the children and Grandchildren and Maggie's mother. Julie would be maid of honor and Cris would serve as best man. They would take a late honeymoon in June to France. The wedding was set for early December and the whole family was looking forward to spending this Christmas together at Rosebriar.

CHAPTER 16

They were both just partially aware of the beautiful surroundings of the church as they stood at the altar enclosed in only their existence. Their own happiness. They had waited so long for this day, their wedding day, and to spend the rest of their lives together. Their eyes stayed fixed on each other throughout the wedding vows, and the children were captivated with the flow of love that existed between their parents.

After the wedding was over the small party went to the new Spanish style home of Jess and Maggie for a reception. The newlyweds were delighted to show off the home they had designed to their children, grandchildren and Maggie's mother. None of them had seen it yet, except for Cris who had helped with some of the building of it, and Julie, who had helped Maggie pick out some of the furnishings.

All of them were in awe when they came into the large front court yard, before entering the Spanish style door of the home. Jess swooped Maggie up and carried her across the threshold of their new home while the family laugh over the surprise look on Maggie's face. He put her down and kissed her passionately while the family clapped their hands and hollered.

Inside, the home was all opened throughout the huge living room, dinning room and kitchen. There was three bedrooms each with their own bathrooms and walk in closets. They would share a large office. Maggie had already moved all of her belongings here, but both she and Jess had vowed not to consummate their relationship this time until they were married.

Jess put more wood in the fireplace, and the family relaxed around the living room, enjoying the finger food that Julie and Lorie had put together and a three tier small wedding cake that was made by a friend.

"Hear ye, hear ye," Jonathan said loudly, as he lifted his glass full of champagne to toast the newlyweds, "I wish all the blessings in the world on both of you and this family forever and a day."

Some of the others joined in with their toast and even the younger members gave their wishes for their grandparents with a sparkling grape juice. After visiting and eating for three hours and watching the wedding gifts being opened, Julie suggested to everyone that they should leave so the newlyweds could be alone. Jonathan and his family were spending the weekend at Rosebriar so that he and Cris could watch a big football game on TV, and Julie and Lorie wanted to go shopping in Sacramento. The four teenagers had plans too, and Bobby was looking forward to watching the football game with his dad and uncle.

" That was a wonderful time we had today with the family. I'm so proud of all of them. But," Jess hesitated, "I thought they were never going to leave," he said, as he pulled Maggie toward him where they sat together on the couch, watching the glowing fire in the fire place. She laid her head on his shoulder.

"I was wondering the same thing," she laugh. "I love them all so much and I'm so proud of them too, but I wanted to be alone with you. It's been so long, Jess."

"Too long," he answered. "I need you so much, Maggie." He passionately kissed her, while he unzipped her ecru wedding dress in the back and together they slipped the long sleeve dress off her arms. He begin massaging her breast through her slip and bra.

"I think it's time to go to bed, Jess," she playfully said, as she led him down the long hall into their bedroom. They undressed each other and clung together in a desire they had known before, but had to be surrendered by the forbidden lonely years in between than and now.

Christmas was only two weeks away. Maggie and Jess had been so busy with their new life they had not had time to do any shopping yet. They planned on finally going Christmas shopping together, something they had talked about many times. This was a special time of year for them, because it was this time of year when they had fallen in love many years before.

They had decorated their new home last night and put the tree up. But Christmas Eve would be spent at Rosebriar due to the wishes of the children. It was always a special time at Rosebriar. The weather was getting colder and a light snow was expected in the foothills. The grandchildren were in hopes that it would be deep enough to go sledding and possibly skiing. A ski trip was being planned by the family sometime after the first of the new year to spend four days at a ski resort in Colorado. Jess and Maggie had decided they were too old to start skiing now and would stay home and work because they would be leaving in June for Paris, France for two weeks.

They drove into Sacramento to get a better selection of toys, games and sports equipment for the grandchildren. As they walked along the street in front of the huge shopping mall where they had shopped together years before, Maggie held Jess' hand.

"It's like we've never been apart, Jess. Like the lonely years have just disappeared. Except we look older. A few more lines and wrinkles, a few more grey hairs."

"Darling, you're just as beautiful to me as ever, and probably more precious to me than ever after all we've been through." He put his arm in hers. "My wife".

They walked through the crowded store and found the toy department. They played with the talking toys and the animated toys. They laugh and teased each other like a couple of teenagers. They picked out several nice toys for Bobby and a large teddy bear for the coming baby's nursery.

"Oh!" exclaimed Maggie, "We don't want to forget the toys to go with the Christmas basket."

"And whose getting the basket this year?" asked Jess.

"A family that the father is dying of cancer. He can't work now and has no insurance. Several businesses in town are planning events for fund raisers to help pay for medical expenses," Maggie answered.

"Gosh, that's terrible the father is dying. We are so fortunate, Maggie. So far our family has been in good health. And they all have a good career. I pray God lets it continue that way."

"I pray that too, Jess. Nothing is for sure or stays good forever. It's the law of nature that bad things happen sometimes. We just have to put it in God's hands."

"Yes, that's for sure," Jess answered.

"The children in that family are all teenagers, so why don't we go to the sports department and get gifts for them and our teenager grandchildren." Maggie suggested.

"Well, let's get that done. And then I want to take you for a prime rib dinner at that restaurant we went to years ago. Remember when our friends from home almost caught us together there."

Maggie turned around with a pleading look in her eyes. "Jess, would you change prime rib for me?" she asked. "I want to do something else."

"Well, sure hon, anything your heart desires."

"Do you think that little German coffee shop is still here? You know, the one that we first ate in together years ago."

"We can find out," he answered.

"I doubt if they have prime rib there. Is that okay?"

"Sure, I'll settle for something else. We can always have prime rib at a lot of places."

They were in the sports department for over an hour trying to decide what presents to get for all the teenagers, before they found the German coffee shop they had went to so many years before. It hadn't changed much. It was still dimly lit with its thick wooden tables and chairs and booths along the back area. It still looked Medieval, like it was somewhere back in the middle ages of Germany.

Christmas music was again playing softly throughout the restaurant, and Maggie remembered how nervous and scared she had been so long ago when she and Jess had came here. She also remembered how much in love she had been with him, how excited she was about these new feelings that she had no right to.

They sat down at a booth and he took her hands in his, "Well, here we are, darling. Is it as exciting to be with me now as it was back than."

"Oh yes, Jess, and I don't have to have those guilt feelings now. I'm so happy we waited and did all we could for Adrian before we got to this point. I know we wasted a lot of years, but it was for the best and we have the rest of our lives together."

They ordered some German food that sounded good and than continued holding hands across the table. It was as though neither one of them could stop touching each other.

"Darling, I hope you never get tired of hearing me say I love you," he told her.

"Never. Do you remember what you said to me here so long ago?"

"Hum—not word for word," he answered.

"Well, I do. You said, I'm crazily and madly in love with you. I don't want just a passing affair. I swear to you I have never had an affair. I had no desire for anyone until you."

"Yes, I remember that. And you said you believed me, and you wouldn't be here if you didn't think that I wasn't honest about it."

He touched her cheek, "Why didn't I meet you before Adrian? We could have had all these years together. Right after I married Adrian I knew I didn't really love her. It was just an infatuation I felt toward her."

"But than we wouldn't have our children that we love now," Maggie answered. "We made our choices, Jess. And everything we do we get a learning experience from it."

"You're right, we should have no regrets," he answered. "Everything happens for a reason. Even though we sometimes don't understand why things happen."

The waitress came and filled their coffee cups and brought them the Black Forrest cake they had ordered for desert.

"Umm, this is good," Maggie said. "I'll have to try making this at home."

"I can see right now you're going to have me so roly poly I won't be able to wrestle those horses and cows to doctor them."

"No, I don't cook that way all time. Just once in awhile. Oh, but I can't wait to get over to France and try the food there. I hear it's wonderful, especially in Paris with all the cafes."

"I can't wait either," Jess sounded anxious, "but we still have six months to wait. I know being married to you the time is going to go very fast from now on . And I don't want it to. I want to savor every minute we have together."

"Oh, darling, I love you," said Maggie, as she leaned across the table and kissed him gently.

Snow covered the landscape at Christmas in the foot hills. The beautiful pine and spruce tree branches drooped downward with the glistening white snow. No matter how many times Maggie had seen snow before, it always struck her as one of the most magnificent things she would ever see. And it was always awesome at Rosebriar.

Maggie and Jess picked up her mother at the senior home and arrived at Rosebriar at about the same time Jonathan, Lorie and the boys did. Julie had the house decorated exceptionally nice this year with Christmas trees in almost every room downstairs. Garland, holly, and pine cones were interweaved with huge gold ribbons, over the mantel and up the staircase banister, and also through the center of the large dinning room table.

It got quite noisy with the teenagers, young adults, and some of their friends greeting each other, plus Bobby trying to get their attention. The kids all went into the family room to play pool or watch the football game on television, while the men stayed in the living room to watch the game. The women gathered in the kitchen to attend to the last minute cooking of the dinner. This was the first year that Julie made the chestnut and liver stuffing and cooked the turkey entirely by herself.

"Oh, it looks great, Julie. Scrumptious. It has my mouth watering," Maggie told her.

Maggie's mother and Lorie agreed. All the women had to do was mash the potatoes, make the gravy and set the table with the good china and silver. And wait for the football game to end. Jess said grace over the Christmas dinner and was amazed as he looked over the different platters and bowls of scrumptious food that set on the huge table.

"My goodness, I've never seen more pleasing, luscious looking food before on one table," he commented.

Cris laugh, "Dad, these ladies know how to cook, believe me. I never ate so well until I married into this family. And now it's your turn."

Maggie added, "Well, we have to give Zelma credit too. She made several of these dishes for us. And also taught Julie and Lorie a lot about cooking."

"Yeah, I've been eating pretty good too since Zelma and Mom taught Lorie how to cook," Jonathan added laughing.

"Well, I sure hope our Christmas basket family is having a nice dinner as well," Julie told everyone.

"They should be," answered Jess, "that basket had everything anyone could want in it and several big boxes of food and presents besides. I'm sure they must be very happy with it."

The rest of the family wanted to know about the family and felt bad about the father having cancer. The talk continued on to the new baby coming next summer. Everyone in the family seemed anxious for it's arrival and what they were going to get it.

"I saved this moment to tell you that it's going to be a little girl. We haven't decided on a name yet, but we are kind of favoring Samantha," Julie told them.

"I can't wait to get my baby sister," Bobby chimed in, while the family laugh.

The talk continued on around the table for another hour while the family discussed high school, college and jobs, and everyone eating until they thought they would pop.

Maggie had never been happier before. She was so proud of Jess and loved him so much. And the family all got along so well, it was almost like Heaven on earth. And with the new baby coming, an answer to prayers, it would be even greater. Did she have too much happiness? Would it end someday she wondered? She wanted it to go on forever.

After dinner there was still several hours of daylight left and the children got the sleds out and slid down the snow on the hills. The adults walked down to the ice covered pond and gazed at the beauty of Rosebriar covered in snow all around them. At dark they gathered back in the house, warming up around the fireplace, and opened their presents .

The next day Julie, Jonathan and their families would spend Christmas at Bill and Lilly's with her children and their families there also. Maggie's mother would attend a party at the senior home, and Maggie and Jess was looking forward to resting at home, maybe even staying in bed most of the day and watching Christmas movies. After all they were still newlyweds.

CHAPTER 17

Maggie brushed her cheek with her hand when she felt something tickling it. She opened her eyes and gazed into Jess' face as he smiled down at her holding a small feather in his hand that he had found on the window sill.

"Wake up sleepy head," he told her, as he cupped her left breast through her silk gown, gently pulling it out of her gown, he pressed his mouth to it circling the nipple with his tongue. "We need to get an early start if we're going to walk around Paris today," he said, but continued to manipulate her warm breast.

"Hum----," she stretch, "I'm so tired, Jess. How many days do we have left to see Paris?"

They had arrived in France a week ago and had decided since they had two weeks all together, that they would first tour some other towns and villages before they spent most of their time in Paris. They had arrived late last night at their hotel in Paris on the left bank where the old fashion charm still existed, even down to the window boxes with bright colored pansies, petunias and geraniums.

"Well, we still have six days before we leave. I suppose we could take it easy and relax for a day. Do you have anything in mind, Mrs. Morgan?" He asked, as he laid down beside her fully clothed. Turning her face toward him he gave her a quick kiss, but lingered close waiting for an answer.

"Hum" She stretch again. "It's so nice to wake up with you beside me. I've never been so happy before. I still can't believe we're really married. After years of waiting we're really together again."

"I've never been happier either, Darling."

She turned over toward him. "Jess, we're in Paris, the most romantic place in the world, and I want to be loved wildly and passionately."

He quickly obliged her by stripping out of his clothes and slipping under the cool sheets next to her soft warm body. Rising above her, his lips met hers lingering on down to her neck and shoulders, while caressing and stroking her most intimate parts. Their passion mounted without music or candles, just the existence of pure love between two people. Than she moaned with pleasure while they both escaped into an untamed exhilarated fulfillment they had only known together when they were younger.

"Darling, I love you so," he whispered.

Their damp bodies encircled each other and Maggie snuggled closer to him feeling like a young women again. "I love you too, so very much," she whispered back.

They had both fallen asleep exhausted, not only from making love, but from the week of traveling around France, and woke up around one o'clock that afternoon.

"Jess, wake up, I'm starved," Maggie pleated, while rubbing his back. "Let's shower and dress and go find our first meal in Paris."

He muddered something that she didn't understand and sat up looking at the clock. "I think they serve a continental breakfast, but I guess we missed it. Probably too late."

Their room was a bit small, but was very nicely furnished and warmly decorated. They had a very small balcony overlooking the street and a view of the Eiffel Tower. A vase of fresh flowers graced the coffee table. The scent of the yellow roses in it added to the romance of being in Paris.

They found a small brasserie which looked inviting and decided to have a quick lunch there, ordering a selection of charcuterie and cheeses. Jess had espresso, while Maggie had her coffee with steamed cream. It wasn't too crowded being the middle of the afternoon, and dress was casual but in style. Most of women wore skirts or dresses with high heels or sandles. No sneakers or blue jeans, as is so popular in America. They had checked with their travel agent on clothing, among other things, so they knew what to pack.

They stood looking up at the Eiffel Tower. "It's more powerful and grand than I ever expected it to be," Jess announced.

"Yes, it doesn't look this big in pictures," answered Maggie.

They took the stairs up to the third deck and than the elevator to the top. The view was beautiful and they tried to pick out landmarks from the Plan de Paris booklet they had purchased to help them get around the city.

They walked through the Champ de Mars and on to the Louvre, where they spent the rest of the day viewing the paintings, sculptures, furniture and objects D' Art. There was so much to see and do in Paris they were overwhelmed by all the attractions, and knew they probably wouldn't be able to go to all the places they wanted to.

By eight o'clock they were hungry again and looked for a nice restaurant to eat in. Most of the eating places posted their menus outside of their establishments. They found one with an antipasto buffet and traditional French food which they decided they would try. It was not too over crowded and they indulged themselves with gourmet food for the next two hours. They knew the meals in France was a sacred ritual, as Parisians give their meals undivided attention. It was a disgrace to diverge from the normal course and rush through a meal. It was after ten o'clock when they finally finished with coffee and than headed back to their hotel to get a good nights sleep and make plans for tomorrow.

Maggie donned a bright yellow stripped sundress with lace edging and matching sandals. Jess wore a pale yellow shirt to blend with her dress, and tan slacks. This was their fifth day in Paris, so today they were going to try to relax at the Luxembourg Gardens with a picnic from a bistro and people watch. In the past three days they had been to the Arc de Triomphe at the top of the world's most famous avenue, the Champs Elysees, and watched as the flame was rekindled that evening in honor of the unknown soldier buried beneath the archway; to the Musee de la Mode et du costume, which had exhibits on clothing design, that Maggie was very interested in seeing. They tried to see most of everything in one section of the city at a time, but there were so many museums, art galleries, shopping centers, luxury fashion boutiques and churches, that to see everything in one week was next to impossible.

This evening they planned a boat trip on the Seine where they would be served dinner, and tomorrow they had tickets at the Opera Garnier. They were both wore out and they hoped the rest today would be good and rejuvenate them.

"Paris is all I ever expected it to be," Maggie told Jess where they sat on a park bench. "I never expected to see so many monuments and fountains and medieval streets and great boulevards in my life. I'm truly in love with it," she went on while munching on an apple.

"I knew you would love it. From the first time I fall for you I knew I had to take you to Paris. The city of romance."

"Oh Jess, quit teasing. You didn't think that."

"Yes, I did. I knew someday I would swish you away to Paris. If we didn't have children and grandchildren we may even move here," he told her smiling while his grey eyes danced.

"I think I would like to live here. The Parisians are friendlier than I expected them to be. From things I've heard I thought they would be kind of uppity to tourist, but they're not."

"Well that little translation book helped a lot . I would still be stuck on 'bonjour' without it. The Parisians do try to help in a situation. I can appreciate that," Jess told her.

"And the food, Jess, have you ever had such delicious food as that roasted duck last night with the orange creme sauce? I have to try to make that sometime."

He laugh at her. "It's a good thing we don't have a tendency to gain weight, because we would have put on ten pounds the way we've been eating."

"I think the walking is keeping the pounds off. I've never walked so much in my life. I have two blisters to show for it. You're probably use to it going to ranches and working on horses and cattle all time."

"We've seen most of the best sights in Paris now so we won't walk much more, but we need to finish some of our shopping for the kids. And I want to go back and purchase that painting that you liked at the Viaduc des Arts."

On the first half of the flight home they both slept. The long days of sightseeing and shopping had worn them both out. Maggie woke up and watched the ocean below. Miles and miles of nothing but water. She reminisced back over the last two weeks. She would always remember France as one of the happiest times in her life. The boat trip on the Seine had been beautiful, an unforgettable experience, as well as the French culture and the centuries of history there. The art work of Monet and Pissarro, the colorful gardens of Paris. It was all so overwhelming and Maggie wanted to remember every single detail of it.

And Jess had been so wonderful she thought, as she looked at him sleeping in the seat next to her. She touched his hair which was greyer now than when they had first fallen in love. It use to be just a light salt and pepper, but now it was more white with light and dark grey streaks. If every husband treated their wives like Jess treats me she thought, this would be a wonderful world. Sometimes she wondered if this happiness she had was too good to be true. She was scared it may not last .

Her thoughts went back to Paris and to the fashion shows she was able to attend there. She didn't particularly like some of the styles by top designers. But then most of these fashions were made for the elite, for top social and political partying around the world. She was glad her designs were doing well through the years, but she was also glad they had not become to well known as to make her a cellebrity to the well meaning, but hounding news media. She had no desire to become a well known fashion designer. She only wanted to live peacefully and have the privacy that she always cherished.

Jess started to stir, and Maggie noticed the plane was starting to descend. She looked out the small window and saw the Statue Of Liberty. They would land in New York and than fly on to Denver, before landing at home in Sacramento.

"Jess, we're almost ready to land in the states. Look at the Statue of Liberty. It's beautiful," Maggie commented, as a thrill went through her. She had been to New York several times before, but it was always exciting looking down on it from above in an airplane.

Rubbing his arm that had went partially asleep while he slept, Jess opened his eyes looking down below. "Yes, it is beautiful, and it's good to be back in the states."

When they arrived home it was a hot day in July and it took several hours to cool the house down again. They called Julie and Cris to see if everyone was alright.

"Mother, I've grown huge in the last two weeks," Julie told her, "all I do is waddle around, and I still have over a month to go yet."

"I can't wait to see you," Maggie told her. "I know the last two months are miserable, especially in the hot summer."

"Cris wanted to put a swimming pool in. You don't care do you, Mother? We thought it would be a good idea."

"No, that sounds great, as long as we can come and swim in it. I hope you put a secure fence around it for the children though."

"We are. It's going to be very secure and locked unless we are in it. The men are working on the pool now, and we decided to put it in the area in back that we had all discussed before when we thought about putting one in."

"Oh, to the east of house, so that the sun can warm the water in the morning."

"Bobby is so excited about it. I probably won't get to go into it until after the baby is born," Julie sounded disappointed.

"Well, that time is going to go fast. I want you to stay home from the shop most of the time now and get plenty of rest. Spoil Bobby, because he won't be the baby much longer. I'm going to work full time at the shop until you're ready to go back to work. Take a month or two after the baby comes and than you can just start back part time for awhile."

"I have to start looking for a nanny for the children. But I probably won't start her until I go back to work."

"I would like to help some with the children too, because I only want to work four or five hours a day after you're back. Than, Julie, you need to only work four or five hours a day also until the baby is older. Jennifer and the other manager can handle things for the time being. Of course we'll have to give them and increase in salary, but it will be worth it."

"That sounds good. Bobby loves you and Jess so much. And you're going to have your first little granddaughter, Mom. How about that?" Julie asked, excited.

"I can't wait. You should see the darling Christening gown I brought her from Paris."

"Oh Mother, really, from Paris, wow."

"We brought you all presents. We'll bring them over in a day or two. We are completely exhausted, and need to rest up for a day."

"Have you heard from Jonathan or Lorie?" Maggie asked. "And how is your father doing? I've been kind of worried about him. He look so tired the last time I saw him. I think he's working to hard trying to keep up Lilly's ranch and working some at Rosebriar too."

Well, to answer your first question. Your son and his family are just fine. I talked to Lorie a few days ago and she said the boys are getting ready to start school and football practice. They all went to the Grand Canyon while you were in France and had a great time. And her and Jonathan are remodeling the office, making it larger. He just won a big criminal case and she said he's getting calls from all over. He may hire another attorney."

"Oh, that's fantastic. I'll have to call them."

"And as far as Dad is concerned, I talked to Lilly several days back, and she said she's trying to get him to slow down and hire some help at their ranch. She did say though that he had went to the doctor for a check up and everything was okay. His blood pressure was just a slight bit high, but the doctor said nothing to worry about, and he changed his medication."

"Well good, I guess he just needs to rest more, but you know your dad, he works from sun up to sun down. Jess is almost as bad, but he has slowed down a lot since we got married."

"Well, I guess he had to, being a new bridegroom and all," Julie teased. "How was Paris? Did you both enjoy it?"

"Oh, we're in love with Paris. If we didn't have all you kids, we decided we would move there," Maggie laugh, and told her about some of the things they did there, which took another hour, until Julie said the baby was pushing on her bladder and she just had to go.

CHAPTER 18

At five a.m. the phone rang loudly, making Maggie jump at once out of bed, as she had been expecting Julie to go into labor anytime. Sure enough it was Cris saying they were leaving for the hospital. Maggie woke Jess, and told him they had to dress and go to the hospital. Maggie was with Julie and Cris in the delivery room after five hours of intense labor on Julie's part. Jess waited all that time in the waiting room and cafeteria, bringing back food for Maggie and Cris. He had to leave that evening to go to Nevada for a Veterinarian conference for several days.

Julie was having a hard delivery and Cris looked so worried trying to comfort her. Maggie assured them both that everything was okay, sometimes it just takes awhile. Maggie was feeling every pain her daughter was having, wishing she could take her place and bear the pain for her. All of sudden with a big push a little girl was born with black hair and bluish-grey eyes.

"Oh, she's beautiful," whispered Maggie.

Cris gave a sigh of relief, while Julie smiled, and dropped off to sleep exhausted. After the nurse cleaned the baby she handed her to Maggie, who had already motioned for Jess to come into the delivery room. Along with Cris they were all three in awe looking at this beautiful baby girl, until the nurse whisked her off to the nursery until Julie was in her room and awake. Jess and Maggie went home to get some sleep before Maggie had to drive him to the Sacramento airport to catch his flight to Nevada.

Before going to the airport they went to the hospital to see how Julie and the baby were doing. They stopped at the nursery window on their way out to get one more look at their new granddaughter.

"She's part of us, Maggie, both of us. She has our blood running through her veins. It's almost like having our own child."

"I always wanted your baby, Jess," Maggie said, putting her arm around his arm. "Isn't she precious? I just never dreamed that our children would get married. That this would happen in our lives."

They stood silent for awhile watching the baby sleep. "Well, we better go if I want to catch that nine o'clock flight."

"I'm going to miss you, Grandma," Jess told her when they got to the airport.

"Not as much as I'll miss you," Maggie said, and raised her head up to kiss him.

He kissed her gently. "Don't forget I'll always love you."

"Jess, don't say it like that. You sound like you'll never be coming back."

"If I never came back my life had been so enriched, Maggie, because of you. Don't worry I'll always be with you."

She watched him go through the boarding door and felt a loneliness she had never encountered before, even though he had to leave her many times to go on his way before they were married. She shook off the feeling, blaming it on the fact this was the first separation since they were married. He would be back in four days she told herself.

The next few days were very busy getting everything ready for Julie and the baby to come home. Maggie made formula for the baby and got the bassinet ready. She put clean sheets on the bed and made a big pot of stew to last them several days. She would be staying with them for a few days until Julie was strong enough to do things. Zelma was still there to help with the cooking and housework, but had taken off while Maggie was there, to visit her family. Julie had obtained a nanny for the children, but she wouldn't start until Julie was ready to go back to work. Jennifer was running the shop until Maggie was able to come back.

Maggie straightened the house up before she picked Julie and the baby up at the hospital. Cris and Bobby were not too messy leaving things lay around, but she wanted everything to look perfect when Julie arrived home. Cris was out in the orchards working, as this was their busy season, and Bobby would be home from school later.

When they got home from the hospital Cris was waiting in the house for them. He had showered and changed clothes so that he could hold his new daughter and get to know her. Bobby had begged Maggie to pick him up at school that day so he would not have to ride on the long bus ride home and could see his new sister that much sooner. It was a delight watching Bobby make over his little sister, and Cris was like a brand new father, even though he had two teenagers and Bobby.

Jess called everyday to check on everyone at home and said things were going well at the conference. He had been scheduled to speak for an hour each day and was enjoying visiting with the other veterinarians, but missed her terribly he said.

She recalled the uneasy feeling she had when he boarded the plane. She shook it off and kept busy taking care of the baby and the family. Zelma returned to Rosebriar and was delighted with the new baby and how Maggie had taken care of the house and the cooking. Maggie returned to her own home. It was on the fourth day and she would have to pick Jess up at the airport later in the evening.

The door bell rang, and when she opened it Cris entered with a bewildered look on his face. "Cris, what is it?" she asked, in a shaky voice.

"Maggie, it's dad." He put his arms around her pulling her close. "His plane crashed after leaving Nevada," he said, his voice wavering.

"No, I have to go pick him up. I was just leaving," Maggie told him insecurely. "I have to go now, Cris."

"Maggie," he held onto her tighter. "Dad isn't coming back. His plane crashed. He died in the crash, Maggie."

Cris broke down into sobs and Maggie knew it was true even though her mind told her not to believe it. She tore loose from Cris. She couldn't comfort him because she felt hopeless, powerless, and a scream built up in side her even though she tried to hold it, she couldn't hold back the hysterical noises from her throat.

"No, No," she screamed over and over again. "Not Jess, no God, not Jess."

Cris tried to console her while feeling helplessly in shock himself. They both knew nothing would ever be the same again without Jess. Part of their world had crumbled, had fallen apart. He was the pillar of their family.

Cris tried to get Maggie to go back home with him, but she wouldn't. She told him she just wanted to be alone. Julie called to see if they were alright. She wanted her mother to come home also, but Maggie wouldn't budge and said she would call them later. That she would be okay. Cris stayed another hour with her until they were both over the first initial shock.

After Cris left, Maggie wondered into their bedroom. Jess would never be here to share this bed with her again she thought. She ran her hand across the smooth Cherry wood of the dresser. They had picked this bedroom set out together. They both fell instantly in love with it when they laid eyes on it, and knew it was the one they wanted. Now she would never part with it. They had made love in it and there were so many wonderful memories. She wondered on throughout the house, their home, that they designed and built together, and bought each piece of furniture together.

"Oh Jess, it can't be true, you can't be gone," she sadly said. "What will I do without you. I can't go on without you."

She had never known such happiness after they were married. When he slipped up behind her while she was preparing breakfast on the weekends, which was the only time Jess had time for a quiet breakfast at home, she would feel him circle her waist and gently kiss the back of her neck cradling her in his arms, and she knew she was loved so much. To wake up at night and feel Jess' body curled around her. To giggle with him over something funny that one of them did. Watching his eyes sparkle when he teased her. Than he would take her in his arms and kiss her tenderly. Yes, she was so content and happy, and now all that was gone, never to be again. Had she waited all those years for him to have only the last ten months of happiness. She knew it wasn't in vain, because these last months were the happiest of her life. There had been a lot of lonely years before for both of them, but still she had loved him all those years and he had loved her.

She flung herself across their bed and cried herself to sleep. She awoke with the doorbell ringing and ringing. She hesitated about answering it, but thought it might be some of the family as the realization hit her that Jess was dead. Julie was at the door.

"Mother, I came to get you. You have to come home with me. We need you, and you need us. I don't want you to be alone right now." Julie said putting her arms around Maggie.

"Oh Julie, I can't believe it's true," Maggie told her crying. "We just got married. We were so happy. Why did this happen?"

"I know it's devastating. Our family will never be the same again, but we have to go on living the best we can, Mother."

They talked awhile longer and Maggie packed enough clothes for several days to stay with the family at Rosebriar. The family found out that Jess had decided to return back to California with two other veterinarians, who were friends of his, on their small private plane which crashed. All three were killed, and the reason of the plane going down had not been found yet.

There were so many arrangements to make and flowers to pick out for Jess' funeral. Maggie's doctor gave her sedatives to help her sleep at night. She gladly excepted the escape to break free from unpleasant realities. At the service it seemed that the whole county turned out to bid farewell to their longtime veterinarian. Most of it was a blur to Maggie as she struggled through the days before, during, and after his funeral. It also seemed that the phone wouldn't quit ringing at Rosebriar or at Maggie and Jess' new home when she returned there. She was grateful that everyone wanted to share in her loss of Jess, but she really didn't feel like talking to anyone just yet. She wanted to reminisce in her memories of him, to draw him close and hold on to him. To be able to cry when she wanted, and not be told that 'things would get better, it just takes time'.

Jennifer told her that she would watch the shop as long as she and Julie needed her to. What would she do without Jennifer. She had been such a good friend and employee through all these years.

After some weeks Maggie decided to sell the home that she and Jess had built and move back to Rosebriar. There was plenty of room at Rosebriar, and Julie and Cris wanted her to help them raise Bobby and Jessica. Yes, Jessica. The family had decided to name the new baby after Jess instead of the one they had chosen. Maggie was delighted and knew Jess would be very happy if he knew.

In the days that followed Maggie often felt his presence. She wondered if Jess' death was punishment for their sins. She had known his love, a love that had sustained her for almost twenty years and now she had only the memory of it. Memories she would never give up. Memories to keep her company for the rest of her days. Memories without him.

The End